THE CHRISTMAS CONTRACT

LARSSON SIBLING SERIES
BOOK 5

EVIE MITCHELL

THUNDER THIGHS PUBLISHING

Editor: Nicole Wilson, Evermore Editing
http://www.evermoreediting.wixsite.com/info
Cover illustrations: Laras Putri

ACKNOWLEDGEMENT OF COUNTRY

I acknowledge the Traditional Custodians of the lands on which I write, the Ngunnawal people, and pay my respect to elders both past and present.

I acknowledge the continued and deep spiritual relationship of the Australian Aboriginal and Torres Strait Islander peoples' to this land, and their unique cultural and spiritual relationships to the land, waters and seas and their rich contribution to society.

Always was, always will be.

To my glorious Greedy Readers!
This series started because you wanted more Erik.
Thanks for joining me on this ride, I hope you loved
every word!

And as always, to my husband.
2020 was batch crazy and yet, here we are.
Together.
Happy.
Still in love.
If that isn't an achievement, I don't know what is!

CONTENT WARNINGS

The Christmas Contract contains explicit consensual sex, consensual punishment, consensual domination, dirty talk, educational issues and failures, struggles with future, discussion of murder mysteries and true crime, anxiety.

If you have any concerns, please email me at EvieMitchellAuthor@gmail.com.

THE CHRISTMAS CONTRACT

Astrid

I forgot to tell my family I wrote a novel.

I didn't think it would be that big a deal. Then a big-name movie star raved about it and suddenly my face is splashed across morning talk shows, and producers are offering me millions for film rights.

Enter Robert 'Robbie' Huynh — Astipia's rom-com heartthrob. He's tall, dark, handsome, and Australian. He's like all my weaknesses rolled into one delicious package.

He's also the one who started this mess, and he wants my film rights. He wants them real bad.

So we strike a deal; I'll sign the contract if he gives me full creative license.

It seemed like a good idea at the time. Only this Christmas contract? It's got all the strings attached.

Robbie

I'm in a rut. An acting rut. Being typecast as the romantic lead is getting old real fast. I want action, adventure, mystery.

I want Astrid Larsson's film rights. And I'm not above using a little Aussie charm to get it.

Only Astrid's not at all what I expected. For a woman who writes crime thrillers, I expected someone hard, seasoned, rough. She's the exact opposite, and she's getting under my skin — big time.

I need to keep my head in the game. After all, this Christmas, all I really want is... Astrid?!

Warning: This book is inspired by Christmas movies, true crime podcasts, and a crisp Aussie accent. So, get thee a man, some mistletoe, and settle in — this read will have you jingling all the way to the bedroom.

PROLOGUE

Robbie

I knocked urgently on the door, praying that behind it would hold the answer to my salvation.

A woman tugged it open, her long brunette hair falling gently to one side, a ready grin on her face. It froze in place when she caught sight of me.

"Sorry to interrupt," I began, forcing a smile on my face. "But—"

"Holy mother of God. You're Robbie fucking Huynh." The woman's gaze flicked to the guy behind me. "And... friend?"

I glanced back at Matt, my bodyguard, who stood just down the garden path, the wind battering both of us as he watched my back.

"That's Matt. Look, sorry to interrupt you, but I'm trying to find Liv Larsson. Her former assistant said she might be here?"

The young woman twisted slightly, yelling over her shoulder, "Liv! You have a visitor." She turned back to me. "Come on in. She's in the dining room."

I stepped through, Matt following, as we trailed the young woman. Even in my anxious state, I had to grin at her Thanksgiving-themed sweater. The mustard-colored monstrosity had a dancing cooked turkey wearing sunglasses on the back, with the words *Don't put me at the kids' table* written in a font made to resemble spilled gravy. It was hideous. Absolutely hideous.

I loved it.

"Liv, did you hear me?" the woman called again. "You have a visitor!"

"They better have pie!" came Liv's yelled response.

We followed a hall down and into a main living area, across the lounge, and around a corner, stepping into a comfortable dining room, the back of which had French doors that opened onto a patio that overlooked a canal.

Note to self, look into buying a beach house.

Holding court at the head of an old wooden table sat Liv Larsson, producer extraordinaire and the only woman who could help me.

God, I hope she can help me.

"Robbie? What the dickens are you doing here?" She rose, coming to wrap me in a hug and press a kiss to my cheek.

I returned it, introducing Matt, then took in the food-laden table, the two vacant high chairs, and festive décor.

"Shit. I'm interrupting. Sorry, I'll just—"

"Nonsense!" An older woman, silver streaking her blonde hair, plonked a bowl of mashed potato on the table. "Sit! Both of you. The more, the merrier." She gestured to the table with a rueful smile. "And it's not as if we don't have enough. I'm afraid we go overboard during the holidays."

"We eat leftovers for at least a month," the woman in the turkey sweater agreed.

"Jemma, he's Robbie freaking Huynh. No doubt he's got better places to be than having dinner with this clan." An older man, his salt and pepper beard trimmed close to his face, his eyes sharp but kind, sat down at the table. "I'm Sune, the father of this motley crew. And I apologize in advance for their craziness, they get it from their mother."

"Excuse me?"

"And that's Jemma, our mother," Liv said waving toward the older woman who now had her hands on her hips as she death-stared her husband. "Take a seat, guys. We can talk after dinner."

Matt and I were quickly added to the table, and I found myself seated beside Liv's sister, the woman wearing the turkey sweater.

She passed me a bowl of green beans. "It's self-serve around here. And you better get in before Rune and Erik make it to the table. My brothers' will eat us out of house and home."

I grinned, accepting the offered bowl. "Thanks for the tip."

The men entered the room trailed by an entourage.

"What? We've already started?"

"That's Erik," the woman said in a hushed whisper, nodding towards the shorter of the two giants. "He's my second oldest brother. Gunnar, my eldest brother, lives down south with his wife."

"And the giant?" I asked, passing her a basket of fresh bread rolls.

"Rune. The baby of the family, if you can believe it. He owns the local bookstore. You should check it out. They do great food and coffee as well."

I filed that suggestion away.

"And you are?"

She laughed, giving me a saucy wink. "Astrid. But you can call me girlfriend."

I grinned, enjoying her easy, no-strings-attached teasing. "Astrid. Rune, Erik, Gunnar, Liv... I sense a Nordic theme."

She lifted one shoulder in a half-shrug. "Dad and Mom are old school. They like to keep some traditions alive and Nordic names are one way they can do that."

She waved at the two women who were settling young children into high chairs. "Gabby is holding Ulf, and Laura is holding Leif. They're Erik's kids."

"I've met Laura."

She slapped her forehead, rolling her eyes at herself. "Of course! Sorry, I forgot that guys work for the same production company."

Not for long, I hope.

Matt leaned over. "I just want to say, this food is fucking ace."

"Thanks. I did absolutely nothing but buy the drinks," Astrid said with a chuckle.

"Where's Nan?" Liv asked, cutting a huge chunk of pie for herself.

"Toilet. She'll be here in a moment. Where's Ian?" Jemma asked, settling at the table.

"On his way. Shouldn't be too far."

Laura set two bowls of mashed vegetables before the kids. "Let's see how long this—"

A spoonful of squash arched across the table, slapping me on the cheek.

"Oh, God! Robbie! I'm so sorry!"

I laughed, reaching for a napkin. "Don't worry about it. Kids will be kids, right?"

On either side of me, Matt and Astrid laughed heartily.

"As long as this doesn't end up on social media, I think we're good."

Astrid pursed her lips together, tipping her head to one side as her eyes danced with amusement.

"Definitely not." She gestured at her sweater. "This is too fabulous to be appropriately captured on film, and there's just not enough space at this table to take sneaky images without getting me in the shot."

I chuckled as the anxious tension that had been coiling in my gut loosened.

Don't get attached. She's Liv's sister. Even if she's not crazy (and the sweater really brings that into question), Liv is unlikely to be supportive of you dating her.

Oh, and you don't date. Remember?

"So, Robbie, Matt." Astrid propped her chin on her hands, shooting us an interested but amused look. "Tell me, do bodyguards have to follow you into the toilet when—"

A large burly, incredibly hairy man burst into the dining room, his wild eyes searching the room, zeroing in on Liv.

"Liv Jemma Larsson!" he bellowed, pointing a large finger directly at her. "You need to stop what you're doing and listen to me."

The table fell silent, and I exchanged a startled glance with Astrid.

"Don't worry," she whispered, leaning into me. "It's just Ian, Liv's boyfriend. We're all a little crazy around here."

She grinned, and I couldn't stop the ache that settled in my gut. I tried to categorize it and failed. Perhaps it was regret, or maybe longing. Or some strange mixture of the two, but either way, it left me melancholy and feeling as if I were an outsider looking in.

That's because you are.

"I'll keep that in mind," I whispered back, Astrid's perfume tickling my nose. Vanilla and something spicy.

Under the table, her thigh pressed into mine for a moment before quickly shifting away. A thread of desire unfurled in me at the innocent touch. I shifted in my seat, my cock beginning to stand to attention.

What the hell, Robbie? You're never like this.

"Just so you know, we may be crazy, but we do have a weakness."

"And that is?"

She leaned in, her grin wide, her eyes shimmering with barely contained laughter.

"Pie."

I laughed, turning back to watch the Sasquatch declare his undying love for Liv. "I'll keep that in mind."

"Do. It's the only way to a Larsson woman's heart."

CHAPTER 1

Robbie

I checked myself in the mirror a final time. Black jeans, black sweater, black overcoat. Black, black, black.

Good thing I look good in black.

Cape Hardgrave hardly seemed the place to be concerned with looks, but I was determined that today would be *my* day. The day I landed the film rights to the book I wanted.

The last time I'd been in Cape Hardgrave had been a mere two weeks ago, during Thanksgiving. I'd been chasing Liv Larsson, my producer and the only woman who could help me.

I wasn't one to celebrate Thanksgiving simply because it wasn't something I'd grown up with. I was Vietnamese-Australian. My father hailed originally from southern Vietnam. My mother was a fourth-generation white Australian. I'd moved to Astipia Kingdom in my late teens to pursue acting.

At first, I'd been the token Asian kid, the quirky side character with the funny one-lines. Then I'd managed to land the lead role in a high school comedy. From there, I'd turned into leading man material, Astipia and Hollywood's rom-com heartthrob.

It'd been my worst nightmare.

While other actors got meaty roles in indie films or superhero movies, I'd been stuck playing the romantic lead in movie after movie.

Don't get me wrong, the work was nice, and the films performed amazing at the box office, but to quote the little mermaid, '*I want more*'.

Which led me to Thanksgiving dinner with Liv and her family. She'd quit the production company I'd signed with, Catch-22, and I knew her contract had an option in it– she could take with her any three clients that she'd brought into the business.

Liv had signed me back when she'd been working in the film division. We'd made a movie, it'd exceeded expectations, and then she'd been scuttled across to the failing reality show arm of the company while I'd been dumped into rom-com hell.

Now I needed out. Badly. And, to quote Star Wars, *Liv was my only hope.*

Over turkey and sides, we'd chatted through the options. It'd been slightly awkward as her partner, Ian, had just proposed, there was a baby involved and something about Astrid's hair? I didn't get it, but Liv had been open to helping me escape my contract.

"I want five years," she'd said around a spoonful of gooseberry pie. "And I want you to choose your projects. I want you to find them, hunt them down, and bring me stuff that gets you excited."

"Can you fund it?" I'd asked, a little niggle of concern growing.

Her new fiancé, Ian, had thrown an arm around her shoulder with a laugh, giving her a squeeze. "Aye, she can fund it. She'll have whatever she needs."

Over pie and cider, the sound of football in the background, we'd struck our deal.

It'd been the next morning that I'd found my first project.

In search of coffee and with time to kill before I needed to head to the airport, I'd taken Astrid's suggestion and stumbled into The Literary Academy, the town's local bookstore.

While avoiding fans wanting selfies, I'd buried myself amongst the books, hiding between the shelves, getting lost in tiny hides-holes and pleasant reading nooks. It'd been a wonderland, an escape of simple pleasure.

The book had been in the second-hand section. Shoved in a pile of romance novels and the occasional cookbook waiting to be re-shelved, the cover had caught my attention. Plain black, a gun made from blood, *Shadow Lies* in a semi-transparent font that made it look almost as if it were hiding amongst the black, the author's name, A. N. Strid, in plain white.

I knew better than to judge a book by its cover, and this one wasn't fantastic. But there was something about it that called to me.

I'd picked it up, finding a small, hidden alcove with an armchair, Matt taking a seat not too far away. Sipping my coffee, I'd cracked the book, immediately becoming engrossed in the story.

I decided to kill Ms. Avery on Tuesday at four o'clock.

Hours passed before I'd been forced to abandon my reading to travel to the airport and catch my flight home.

I'd practically rushed to be seated on the plane just so I could dive back in, becoming captivated by the narrative, spellbound by the wicked web of deceit and terror the author had woven. The book had ignited something in me, burrowing it deep. I'd neared the climax as we'd gently landed, the plane bumping along the runway as we taxied towards the gate, me hurriedly devouring every sentence.

I'd stayed on board, the last person on the plane to leave in order to finish that final page.

So spellbound by the story, I'd spent that night imagining the screenplay—with me as the antagonist.

Evil walks among us. Ordinary. Friendly. Affable. It steps into the light with the sole intention of casting a shadow. And that shadow runs deep. It spreads until it blocks all light.

I live only to leave those dark places in my wake.

Around 3.00am I'd given up on sleep and spent the rest of the night scrolling the internet to find the mysterious A. N. Strid. Two days passed, then three, then a week. Despite my best efforts, there wasn't anything to find. The author had self-published. They didn't have a website or social pages, and their bio contained a scant three lines.

> Fan of true crime podcasts.
> Lover of pie and obscure facts.
> Not a murderer.

So, I'd done what any sane person did these days– I asked the internet for help.

@THEOFFICIALROBBIEHUYNH

> Hi internet! Need some help tracking down an author. Anyone have a contact for A. N. Strid? Loved Shadow Lies! Honestly hoping for a sequel. Any info appreciated.

I'd included a picture of me holding the book. While my inbox blew up, within hours a real lead slid into my DMs.

@THEEDITBYJANE

> Hey! OMG! I just wanna start by saying I loved you in The Bro Prince! Anyways, I edited this book. I too thought it was brilliant. Bone-chilling but totally brilliant.

@THEOFFICIALROBBIEHUYNH

> Which was your favorite part?

@THEEDITBYJANE

> Megan at the end. Did you see that coming!? I didn't!

@THEOFFICIALROBBIEHUYNH

> Holy shit! Right!? So you know the author?

@THEEDITBYJANE

Know? Dude, we're like best
friends.

@THEOFFICIALROBBIEHUYNH

You are? Who is it? Can you give
me their details? I need to
contact them!

@THEEDITBYJANE

Sure! Her name is Astrid Larsson.
We were roommates during
college. She asked me to edit it
about six months ago. I didn't
realize she'd published it. Kept
that one quiet lol!

@THEOFFICIALROBBIEHUYNH

Wait. As in Astrid Larsson who
lives in Cape Hardgrave?

@THEEDITBYJANE

That's the one! Last I heard she'd
moved back home.

@THEOFFICIALROBBIEHUYNH

I thought you were best friends?

@THEEDITBYJANE

We were but we lost touch after I
graduated last year.

@THEOFFICIALROBBIEHYUNH

Do you know if she has socials?
Or an email? A phone number
even?

@THEEDITBYJANE

Sorry, no luck. Astrid hates all forms of social media. Shuns it. Probably why you can't find her online. Always said social media was how people found out enough to gain your trust then kill you. I think her cell number has changed but you could try Thor's Shipbuilding. It's her family's business.

One phone call to Thor's Shipbuilding later and I'd discovered that Astrid Larsson was harder to track down than even the most diligent of A-list celebrities.

You could just call Liv. She'd be able to help.

I ignored that little voice, not wanting to bring my new boss in just yet. I wanted to go to her with a complete project. I wanted to impress her.

I needed to impress her.

Which led me to today, to this very moment.

I'm gonna get these film rights. I have to.

I checked myself in the mirror once again, studying my appearance with a critical eye. If I were to convince Astrid to sign over her creation then I needed to look the part.

And look the part I did. With a small smirk, I turned, heading towards the door, Matt falling in beside me.

A. N. Strid, I'm coming for you.

CHAPTER 2

Astrid

"This isn't the book I ordered."

The woman, dressed in a Christmas sweater complete with Rudolph with a flashing nose, glared at me, holding the book out for me to take.

Would it be rude to ask where she got her sweater from?

Her foot began tapping as her arms crossed.

Uh-oh! Abort! Abort!

"Ah, sorry. Let me take care of this for you. Name?"

"Susan Dawson."

"Just a moment."

I began to type her name into the computer

system, searching for her order, but Susan wasn't having it.

"No, I won't wait a moment. Do you have any idea how busy my day is? I have three other stores to get to in the next two hours. I have presents to buy. I have food to purchase. It's nearly the holidays. I will *not* wait a moment! I want my book now!"

I found her order by checking the title of the book.

"Well, Susan, our records show this is the book you ordered. But if you tell me which book you meant to order, I'll—"

"Your records are wrong!" she screamed, her face taking on a red splotchy appearance. "I did *not* order this!"

I sucked in a breath, trying to find some calm.

Why did I let Rune talk me into this? Was it money? Cause surely I don't need cash to live and eat and clothe my body this badly. I could become a nudist hermit who lives on the rays of the sun. Christmas in retail is the worst. I regret everything. Everything.

The little voice that I liked to call Evil Astrid answered back.

You wouldn't be in this predicament if you just told your family about that one teeny-weeny minor detail.

Shit your mouth, you whore.

Susan reached for the book, tossing it on the floor as her screaming kicked up a decibel.

I opened my mouth to interject when Rune, my younger brother, and owner of The Literary Academy, appeared at my elbow.

"Ms. Dawson," he greeted smoothly. "Which book were you after?"

I'm not sure if it was his size (well over six feet), his looks (devilishly Viking handsome), or his tone (calming but no-nonsense), but Ms. Dawson calmed the fuck down.

Huh. How do I learn that trick?

"Oh Rune, this woman—"

"My sister."

Ms. Dawson's eyes widened, her throat moving as she visibly gulped. The pulse in her neck jumped, her carotid artery bulging.

Evil Astrid began whispering in my ear.

There's a pen knife on the counter. If you press it against the tender flesh of her neck, she might squeak.

"Do you know how long it takes to bleed out?" Your lips would graze the shell of her ear as you'd whisper the question. She'd shake her head, too terrified to speak.

"Let's find out, shall we?"

"Astrid!"

I snapped out of my daydream, blinking up

to find Rune's unamused gaze had settled on me.

"Sorry?"

He pressed his lips together, crossing his arms. "I'd ask what you'd done to upset Ms. Dawson, but she's always like that."

I blew out a breath. "Sorry, I'm just a bit...."

"Distracted?"

I nodded, running a hand over my face.

"Astrid, is something wrong?"

You're gonna have to tell them sooner or later.

I looked up into the eyes of my little brother, finding only calm understanding and a lack of judgment.

I'm twenty-seven and currently living in an apartment above my older brother's workshop and temping at my younger brothers' bookstore. I hate architecture and failed my final semester, which means I have to go back and spend more time and money that I don't have to finish a degree I no longer want. I have an obsession with true crime podcasts that has resulted in me manifesting an Evil Astrid voice in my head. I wrote and self-published a novel that hasn't sold even one copy. I dyed my hair, and Mom thinks that means I'm having an existential crisis and... I'm not sure she's wrong.

I pasted a smile on my face, forcing cheer I didn't feel.

"Nope, all good."

You little liar.

"Excuse me? Can someone help? I'm looking for a book."

I kept the fake smile glued to my face, turning to the older woman standing at the counter.

"Sure, I can help. What's the title?"

She squinted at me. "Do I know you?"

"Maybe, I'm Rune's sister."

She shook her head. "No, that's not it."

"Um, I've been working here for a week?"

"No, that's not it either."

I shrugged, my patience beginning to wear thin. "So, your book?"

"Yes, it has a red cover and white writing."

I waited for her to continue, mentally sighing when I realized that was all the info she was going to give me.

"Do you remember what it was about? An author or genre? Anything?"

The woman frowned, glancing around. "Where's Rune?"

My brother had vanished into thin air.

The bastard. Can you smother someone with a book? That seems like a way he'd love to die.

"Probably out back dealing with new deliveries." I gritted my teeth, attempting to maintain my smile. "Did you need him for something?"

"He always finds me the book I want."

I sucked in a deep breath holding it for a count of five, then let it out slowly. "How about I go for a search? See if I can't find this book you were after. Did you see it in this store? Do you remember approximately where? Maybe we can retrace your steps to work it out."

The woman shoved her bifocals up her nose, narrowing her eyes on me. "You had blonde hair."

I raised an eyebrow. "Sorry?"

"In the news article. You had blonde hair."

Great. I'm dealing with a crazy person. Merry Christmas to me.

"News article?" I asked politely.

The woman reached into her massive handbag, rifling through, muttering to herself as she pulled things free, dumping packets of candies, a candle, three tissue packets, and a rather large tube of antacids on the counter.

"Where did I put that darn phone? Always moving about, not where I want it to be when I need it. Useless piece of – here!" She pulled the phone from her bag, holding it up in triumph.

I watched, bemused, as she slowly unlocked it, typing onto the touchscreen with one finger.

"Here we go. This is you, isn't it?"

I took the offered phone, my stomach

bottoming out when I saw myself staring out from the screen.

That's my college ID. Shit, am I a missing person? Wait. Am I dead? Is this the bad place?

I scrolled down, reading the article, beginning to experience an out-of-body moment.

It looks like Hollywood heartthrob and Astipian local Robbie Huynh's search for the mysterious A. N. Strid is over – and in record time! Less than 24 hours after he first tweeted his search, an anonymous fan has come forward to reveal the author.

Astrid Larsson, 27, of Cape Hardgrave, self-published the book online earlier this year. While the Astipian local's novel appears to have languished at the bottom of online rankings, selling less than a hundred copies, it certainly managed to capture Robbie's attention.

"Less than a hundred? More like it didn't sell even one," I muttered.

Robbie reportedly purchased the paperback in the author's hometown, becoming obsessed with the crime thriller. His one tweet now has the book rocketing up the rankings, and based on the heated debates on social media, it's likely Shadow Lies might just become the hottest read of the holiday season.

But why is Robbie so interested in tracking

down the author? Well, word has it, he's after the film rights. For a man who's known for his rom-coms, it's hard to imagine Robbie playing anything other than the hero. Is this his moment to pivot? Or will this gamble flop?

Stay tuned for more updates as they come to hand. Like, share, and subscribe below.

I handed the phone back to the woman in a daze.

"See? That's you, isn't it?"

"Um...."

Shock had rendered me speechless. I pulled my phone from my pocket, needing to verify if this were a joke.

4032 text notifications.

I stared at my screen for a moment, then quickly navigated to my book sales dashboard, unable to comprehend what I was seeing.

206, 509 books sold.

I gulped, my hands shaking as I tucked the phone back into my pocket.

How is this possible? How?

"Excuse me? Astrid?"

My head twisted, gaze landing on the man dressed in all black. The Australian accent, the gorgeous dark eyes, his small cheeky grin, Robbie fucking Huynh was looking at me like he wanted to eat me up.

"Robbie?" I squeaked, fumbling with my phone. "What are... what are you doing here?"

His gaze started at the reindeer antlers gently flashing on my head, dropped to my Christmas wreath earrings, paused on my cherry red lipstick, then continued to my ugly *Home Alone* inspired Christmas sweater before stopping on the candy cane leggings that I'd paired with red chuck tailors.

He finally looked up, a muscle jumping in his cheek as if he were fighting a grin. "You wrote *Shadow Lies*?"

I swallowed as Rune approached looking from me, to the old lady, who watched this entire exchange with unconcealed fasciation, to Robbie, to Matt, Robbie's bodyguard who hovered in the background.

"I...." I swallowed again, my mouth a desert, my heart in my throat. "Yeah. I wrote it."

"*Shadow Lies*?" Rune asked.

"A book. I wrote a book."

Rune started his eyebrows raising. "Sorry, did I hear correctly? You wrote a book?"

I nodded, panic beginning to overwhelm me. "Wow, that's—"

Robbie interrupted Rune, stepping forward to capture both of my hands in his.

"I need the film rights. Will you sell them to

me?" His dark eyes bore into me, pinning me with their intensity.

I stared back, wide-eyed and freaking out.

"You.... What?"

His face softened, a small grin appearing at the corner of his mouth. "Astrid, you wrote a book I want to make into a movie. What do you say?"

I looked from him to Rune, to the old lady, then back.

"No."

CHAPTER 3

Robbie

Okay, today wasn't exactly going to plan.

For one, Astrid wore the most hideously blatant Christmas outfit I'd ever seen. She also looked tired, strung out, and stressed. Dark circles bruised the soft skin under her eyes, her lipstick had been worried mostly away, a perpetual frown marred lines into her forehead, and the tension in her shoulders was evident.

I'd expected tortured artist or the sassy woman from Thanksgiving, not Santa's helper mid-breakdown.

"No?" I repeated.

Astrid withdrew her hands from mine,

stepping back. "That's correct. *Shadow Lies* isn't for sale."

Frustration and desperation bubbled up in me, the combination dangerous.

Patience, Robert. You can do this.

"Astrid, let me apologize for the rude introduction. Let's start over." I held out a hand for her to shake. "I'm Robert Huynh."

She took my hand automatically, shaking it with a frown. "Dude, do you not remember? You came to Thanksgiving."

Well, this is going well.

"I just meant... that is, I thought we could start over."

She made a dismissive gesture. "Look, it's fine. It's nice to see you but I have to get back to work."

"Oh, don't rush on my account." The old lady shoved her glasses up her nose, the bifocals making her eyes look huge. "I'm Maeve, by the way." She held a hand out to me.

I took her offered hand, staring at it awkwardly when she didn't shake but turned it so her knuckles were facing up, holding it as if she were the Queen.

"You're meant to kiss it," she directed with a little push of our joined hands my way.

"Maeve," Rune sighed. "Leave him alone.

He's got enough to worry about without you forcing him to kiss you."

He turned to his sister, crossing his arms and giving her an eyebrow lift. "So, you wrote a book?"

She blushed, looking away. "Yeah."

"And you didn't tell me because...?"

"Because it's not great. It hasn't sold even a copy."

Rune, arms still crossed, moved his hand so his thumb pointed at me. "Um, this guy right here who's wanting to buy your film rights says that's a lie."

She coughed, shaking her head. "Sorry, I should say *hadn't*. Not until yesterday."

"And now?"

She pulled the phone out playing on the screen for a second before handing it over to Rune. He read it letting out a low whistle.

"Astie, this is... you're a bestseller. You're going to be famous."

She audibly swallowed, shaking her head. "I'm not. Honestly, I'm—" she broke off, spinning to look at me. "Wait. Where did you even get a copy?"

"Here. It was in the second-hand section."

Her eyes bugged out. "And you bought it?"

"Uh-huh. Read it in one day." I stepped forward, attempting to close what felt like a chasm between us. "Astrid, it's really good. Being told through the eyes of the antagonist? You think he's one thing and it turns out he's something else? It's like... Jekyll and Hyde for the modern-day."

She frowned. "I'm sorry. What?"

I pulled the copy from my backpack holding it out to her. "Can you sign it?"

Her eyes grew huge, their blue depths swimming. "Again, I'm sorry, what?"

I grinned. "I want it signed. It'll be a collector's item."

She took the offered book, Rune producing a pen. For a second she hesitated, her face taking on a sense of wonder. Then she wrote on the title page, signed it with a flourish, and handed it back.

"I didn't know you were selling these in my store," Rune commented to his sister as I flicked the book over, reading her inscription.

"Um, I wasn't. The book has been out for over six months and no one wanted to read it. So, I traded all my copies in."

"How many?"

"Three. I could only afford to order three author copies originally."

"Did you keep any of them?"

She shook her head. "No. I traded them in

here. I needed the money… and I didn't want to see them."

"Fuck. Stay here." Rune disappeared into the shelves, leaving me with Maeve and Astrid.

I opened the book reading her inscription.

> *Dear Robbie,*
>
> *It feels surreal to write this but thank you for being my number one fan.*
>
> *Granted, you're also my only fan but still, thank you.*
>
> *Your girlfriend, A. N. Strid.*

I laughed, amused she'd remembered our joke from Thanksgiving. "Thanks, girlfriend, but what's the N stand for?"

"Huh?"

I tapped the cover, pointing at the N. "A and Strid is Astrid, right?"

She laughed, nodding. "Yeah."

"And the N?"

"It's for my grandmother, Nan. She's a fellow true crime fan. We listen to podcasts together."

Maeve chose that moment to interrupt.

"Well, this is lovely, but if the boy isn't going

to give me his number then I need to get going. Astrid, do you have that book I was after?"

"The one with the red cover and white writing?"

She nodded.

Astrid's face took on a pink color. "I'm not sure which... um... maybe I can..."

Rune reappeared, two books cradled in his arm, a third in his hand. He handed Maeve the red-covered book. She took one look at it and nodded.

"Yep, this is the one."

She slapped a few notes on the counter then toddled off toward the exit, calling a farewell over her shoulder. Rune handed Astrid the two other books.

"Here."

"Rune...." She took the copies of *Shadow Lies*, placing them on the counter. "At least let me pay for them."

"Nope. But I'll take you signing my first batch when it comes in."

The brother and sister smiled at each other, their familiar love clear.

That ache I only ever experienced around the Larsson's returned like an unwanted and uninvited toothache.

You have everything you could ever want.

Except for these film rights. Just pull it together, man!

"Now," Rune pulled back, waggling a finger at Astrid. "Get back to work, Ms. Author. Today is a madhouse."

Astrid rolled her eyes, catching sight of me still hovering.

"You're still here?"

I nodded. "I'll be here all day until you let me pitch to you."

She shook her head, gesturing at the queue of people. "You're gonna be waiting a while."

My resolve hardened. "Surely you'll have a lunch break at some point."

She considered me. "If you pay, I'll listen. I'm not promising anything, though."

"Done." Triumph had me smiling. "I'll even pitch in and help. I did retail for a few years during my starving artist stage, you know."

She grimaced. "As much as I'd love the help, please don't. You'll cause a riot. Go hide in the shelves, and I'll find you when I'm ready."

With that direction, she turned, jumping back into the hectic craziness of holiday retail shopping, leaving me with a weird sense of anticipation.

To quote Jerry Maguire, show me the money!

CHAPTER 4

Astrid

Christmas movies were nothing but lies. There was nothing good about this time of the year.

Well, not if you worked in retail. I'd once again bought into the lies, wearing the paraphernalia and thinking that this time of year was full of cookies, roasted chestnuts, Christmas trees, and goodwill to all men.

Lies. I called lies on the whole damned thing. There was nothing good about this time of the year, bah humbug!

"—which is why you're going to give me a discount!" The man finished screeching in my face. His core complaint seemed to be centered around a spelling mistake he'd found in a traditionally published book.

"Well, sir, as you would be aware, we are not the publishing company. I would be more than happy to give you a refund, however, we can't—"

"I want it fixed! Today! I can't gift this to someone with a mistake in it."

I gritted my teeth, attempting to paste a smile on my face. "Sir, please, as you can understand—"

"I said I want a new book! Corrected! Now!"

Spittle flew through the air landing on my cheek. We both stared at each other for a beat, his gaze dropping to the large wad on my skin.

"Dude... ew. Seriously, so uncool." I reached under the counter finding an antibacterial wipe and quickly cleaning my cheek. "I think you'd better leave."

"But what about my—"

My patience snapped. I suddenly understood why someone might commit murder.

"Sir, it's time to go. You can come back when you're ready to be calm."

"Excuse me, I—"

"Good day to you, sir." I snapped.

"But—"

"I said, good day!" I crossed my arms, glaring over the counter.

Behind him, the line of customers was a mix of eye-rolls, amusement, or sympathetic smiles as they watched me deal with this crazy man.

With a final bluster, he gathered his things and stormed from the counter, heading towards the door, brushing past Rune on his way out.

Rune's eyebrows raised and he shook his head, disappearing back into the shelves.

I should really try not to alienate all the customers in one day.

I managed to serve the rest of the queue without incident, clearly a Christmas miracle with the way this day was going.

"You ready for lunch?" Ashley, my brother's assistant store manager, asked, her shock of red hair, bobbing dangerously as her Santa hat hairclip pulled the precarious mass to one side.

My stomach grumbled in response to her question. She laughed, waving me off, turning to serve a young woman searching for a book on tantric breathing for her anniversary.

Hmm, I wonder if there are books on how to suffocate people.

I forcefully shoved Evil Astrid into a dungeon, sending her to the naughty corner.

Hush you, we can think about that creepy shit when we're not in public.

I went searching through the shelves finding Robbie in one of the small alcoves, his bodyguard pretending to read a book nearby. The guy looked like a linebacker which meant his attempt at blending was failing, big time.

I crept up, leaning on the shelf beside him.

"Hey, it's Matt, right?"

He nodded, holding out his hand to give it a firm shake. "You can go over, he's just rereading."

"Rereading?"

"Mm, your book. He's pretty obsessed. Highlights passages and everything."

I raised an eyebrow, glancing Robbie's way. Sure enough, he was engrossed in my book, the pages marked with post-it notes.

"He's serious?"

"Deadly."

Huh. There you go.

I glanced at Matt, raising an eyebrow. "Have you read it?"

He grinned, nodding. "Forced it on me. It's good. Real good. And I say that as someone who hates reading. That scene with the cops in the sewer?" He shuddered. "Stuff of goddamned nightmares."

Something warm lit in me, a weird fluttering of anxious pleasure.

They liked it. They really, really liked it.

At the same time, for some reason that made me almost panicked. I'd published hoping someone would read my story. Only two people had ever read *Shadow Lies* before I hit publish, that being me and my former roommate, Jane. She'd edited it in exchange for me cleaning the apartment for a month.

I hadn't expected anything special. Maybe one or two sales. But after six months of nothing but crickets, I'd slowly shelved any hope, focusing on my final semester.

Load of good that did me.

"Robbie?"

His head jerked up, his gaze focusing on me.

"Oh, hey. Is it lunchtime?"

God, that accent.

Evil Astrid agreed, letting out a contented purr.

"Um," I cleared my throat. "Yep. Shall we?"

The Literary Academy was split across two warehouses. One held the giant bookstore, the other, connected via a small walkway which Rune had turned into a book tunnel, held the café-slash-bar.

We walked through, Robbie staring up at the walls of the tunnel as Matt trailed us.

"Are these books all real?" He asked, running fingers along the spine.

"Of course. It took Rune over two months to

build it. He made us all pitch in, even Liv. Though it would have taken half the time if she'd not accidentally destroy a quarter of it."

"Your family seems close."

A knot formed in my stomach, guilt roiling in my gut. "We are."

"Must be nice."

I glanced his way, raising an eyebrow. "You're not?"

He shook his head. "I was a mistake, the only child of only children. My parents are great, don't get me wrong, but I wasn't in the plans. They did their best but never quite knew what to do with me."

"You moved to Astipia when you were young, right?"

He nodded, his face tilting back as we exited the tunnel, walking into the warmly lit café. "Yeah. Sixteen, seventeen. Something like that. They had a friend who was willing to put me up in his spare room."

"What about school?" I asked as we snagged an empty booth, the café hopping with holiday catch-ups.

"I did distance for a while. Graduated and tried to get into the Royal Arts College but that fell over. So I did the poor waiter thing, working as a store clerk at night, going to auditions all day."

I handed him a menu while Matt took a seat at the bar. "And that worked out for you."

He laughed. "Yeah, I got lucky. Ran into Glenn, my agent. He took me on, found me a few small gigs and it grew from there."

"And now you're Astipia's heartthrob."

His face twisted, something passing over it. "Yeah."

Uh-oh. There's a story there.

The waiter arrived, we ordered, then sat awkwardly while Matt watched discreetly from the bar.

"So—"

"Can I—"

We broke off, laughing.

"You first," I said, giving him a nod.

"Can I tell you what I loved the most?"

A blush crept up my neck, heat flushing my cheeks. "Um, sure."

He tapped the book cover, shaking his head. "Megan."

Ah, the protagonist.

"Every moment you were thinking she's nothing but a doe in a hunter's periscope. Then that shift at the end? Phwaww!" he laughed. "Took me by surprise. Took the killer by surprise as well."

A reluctant grin tugged at my lips. "She enjoyed toying with him."

"And you enjoyed toying with the reader."

Yeah, I did.

The entire book was premised on the idea that the narrator was stalking little Megan Somett from 11 Dresden Drive. The murderer, a man, was obsessed with killing her. He fantasized about it as he committed atrocities on others, but never quite got her in the right place to enact the deed.

In the closing chapters it finally happened, the stars aligned and the reader braced for him to finish Megan off... only for Megan to turn around and kill him. The hunter, it turned out, was really the prey.

The waiter returned with our lunch, handing over drinks, hesitating as she served up our plates.

"Um, I hope this isn't rude but... would you mind if I took a photo?"

I turned to Robbie, seeing him nod. "Sure, go right ahead."

"Oh my God, thanks so much!"

She pulled a phone out of her pocket, crouching in front of the table as Robbie shifted, leaning over her shoulder and smiling. I pulled back, moving out of the shot only for the girl to frown, shaking her head.

"Astrid, aren't you going to be in it too? You're famous!"

"Oh... um... sure. I mean. Of course."

I leaned in, pasting a smile on my face, staring into the lens as she clicked a few.

"Thanks so much!" She squealed, cradling her phone. "No one was going to believe me otherwise. Enjoy your lunch!"

She bounced away, disappearing into the crush of diners.

"Does that happen often?" I asked, reaching for my latte.

"Yeah. Multiple times a day."

I shook my head. "I honestly can't imagine that. It seems so intrusive."

He shrugged, digging into his pulled pork sandwich. "Price of fame."

Sucky price.

I scooped up a spoonful of my soup, blowing softly. "You know, even if I wanted to give you the rights, which I don't because the books are always better, there's an issue."

He raised an eyebrow, still chewing.

"Liv." I gave a one-shouldered shrug. "Not that they're for sale but if they were, my sister forever and always gets first dibs."

Robbie scratched his chin. "So, I need to speak to Liv?"

I nodded then shook my head. "Yes. I mean no. It's not going to change anything."

"But I can try?"

I blew out a breath, rolling my eyes. "Look, you can but could you wait? I mean, that is... I haven't actually told them about the book just yet."

"I'm sorry?"

I hesitated, using my spoon to stir my soup. "Umm... I mean... that is to say... um...." I cleared my throat. "I kind of didn't tell them."

"Like... at all?"

I nodded, cringing. "Yeah."

"Oh man," he sniggered. "You're dead meat."

He's not wrong.

"Yeah well, this is all your fault you know." I pointed my spoon at him. "If you'd just left me alone like a normal person—"

"Nope. Not gonna happen. I need those film rights."

"Then I guess we're in a standoff, cause, for the hundredth time, they're not for sale."

He took an aggressive bite of his sandwich frowning at me as he chewed.

"What?" I asked, the trill of my phone interrupting us. I pulled it free, frowning at the unknown number.

"Hello?"

"Is this A. N. Strid?"

"Yes?"

"Hold please."

I frowned as the phone went silent for a

beat then a man's booming voice echoed down the line.

"Is this Ms. Strid?" He asked, his tone jolly.

"Um, yes. Who are you?"

"Bob Taylor, Catch 22 Productions. I want to buy your film rights for *Shadow—*"

I hung up on him, sliding the phone onto the table.

Robbie raised an eyebrow, swallowing his bite. "All good?"

I nodded, glancing at the number as my phone began to ring again.

Unknown number.

I blew out a breath, answering it.

"Hello?"

"Ms. Strid? It's Bob, looks like we were disconnected."

"Nope, I hung up. Don't want to talk to you. Please stop calling."

"Wait! Why? I'm offering you millions here!"

"Dude, I'm Astrid Larsson, my sister is Liv Larsson. You know, the woman you decided not to promote? I don't care how much you're offering me; you can get stuffed."

With that parting snap, I ended the call, slapping my phone back on the table with a huff.

"Was that... Bob?" Robbie asked, his eyes wide.

For an actor, he has zero poker face. He'd never be able to be a serial killer. A victim though....

I hushed Evil Astrid.

"Yeah. Hopefully, he took the hint."

"How much did he offer?"

I shrugged. "Supposedly millions. But nothing is worth my dignity. Or that of my sister."

Robbie finished his sandwich, chewing slowly as he wiped his hands clean on a napkin, considering me with a thoughtful expression.

"What?" I asked, lifting my spoon to my mouth. "You keep looking at me like that."

"If I call Liv right now and got her permission, would you sell me the rights?"

I hesitated for a moment, tempted to lie to him then shook my head slowly. "Sorry, no."

"But why?"

Because I'm a failure. Because I know this wouldn't be a success.

"Because the movie is never as good as the book."

CHAPTER 5

Robbie

I found myself on the abandoned beach, staring into the distance like some discarded lover. The freezing wind whipped at my hair and cheeks but I ignored the chill, determined to clear my head. Even Matt had abandoned me, swearing softly a half hour ago and retreating into our car, watching me from inside the warmth.

On a day like this, even the most diehard of stalkers would be hard-pressed to get out of bed.

Unless you're me.

And therein lay the issue. Ms. Astrid Larsson had turned me into a stalker.

Wind whipped up damp sand tossing it in

my face as the ocean crashed into the shore. My violent emotions appreciated the turbulence of the churning sea and bitter icy wind.

No.

Astrid's overt rejection echoed through my ears, hardening my resolve. I needed her to say yes. I needed her to trust me with this project.

The movie is never as good as the book.

Her reasoning dug into me, niggling, burrowing like a splinter, prodding me to consider the problem from all perspectives.

I need Liv.

Liv Larsson had to be one of the most brilliant producers I'd ever met. She had a mind that I envied, able connect dots to pull at heartstrings in a way few could rival.

It didn't hurt that she also appeared to be Astrid's sister.

I pulled my phone from my pocket, hitting her number.

"Robbie fucking Huynh, what's this I hear about you stalking my sister?"

Ah crap.

"Look, all I wanted was to get a contact. How was I to know her face would end up splashed across news sites?"

I'd woken to messages from my publicist advising that my search for Astrid had gone viral, her face plastered across news sites and bulletins as the image of me and her in the coffee shop with that waitress had appeared.

The confirmation that I'd not only met but was having lunch with the author I sought, had sent the gossip mill a twittering with theories.

Liv made a noise, one I associated with pursed lips, raised eyebrows, and heavy judgment.

Okay, this isn't going well.

I ran a hand over my face, grimacing as I rubbed sand into my skin. "Liv, I need this. You asked me to find a project. This is the one. I want *Shadow Lies.*"

There was a long pause. "Robbie, where are you? You sound like you're in a wind tunnel."

"I'm on a beach."

Another pause. "Exactly *which* beach?"

I glanced at the sign. "Coral?"

Liv huffed down the phone. "Robbie, are you in Cape Hardgrave?"

I winced at her tone. "Um, yes?"

Silence roared down the phone line, her judgment thick.

Eventually, she sighed. "Right, here's what we're going to do. You'll come to my parents' house for dinner tonight. Astrid is going to *finally* announce to the family she's written a novel. We're going to eat my mother's cooking and listen to my father bemoan the weather.

You'll accept the wine my fiancé offers, and won't, I repeat, *won't* mention how I've popped in the last two weeks. Seriously, Robbie, I'm birthing a hippo."

I swallowed a laugh.

"After dinner, Astrid and I will retreat to the study where you will pitch your idea. We will then discuss it and work out if it is the right decision for her. I love you, Robbie. But my loyalty is forever and always with Astrid."

"That's what she said about you."

She chuckled, her voice warming incrementally. "So, you spoke to her first?"

"Yeah. Yesterday."

"And?"

"She turned me down."

Liv barked out a laugh. "Good girl."

"But you'll help me?"

She remained quiet for a long time. "Yes. But only because you sound desperate. Seriously, dude, it's not an attractive attribute. Do better."

I laughed, feeling lighter than I had in days. "Can you text me the address?"

"Will do. Be on time. And bring something. My mother likes flowers."

I hung up, pushing to a stand with a groan, cold muscles tight from disuse. I stretched for a moment then headed back up to the car where Matt waited, listening to a podcast.

"You done?" He asked as I slid into the passenger seat.

"Yep."

"Home?"

I glanced outside, watching as the first heavy drops of sleet begin to fall, dotting the window. Resolve stiffened my spine and I suffered an overwhelming need to see what weird and wacky cardigan Astrid wore that day.

"Actually, you want a coffee?"

Matt chuckled, putting the car in drive. "Is coffee what we're calling it now?"

"No comment."

CHAPTER 6

Astrid

Ambushed. My family had ambushed me.

I'd had the day off and spent it avoiding calls, text and any form of news article.

My family, apparently, had not.

Around the table sat my Nan, Father, my brother Erik and his fiancé, Laura, Rune, and his fiancé, Gabby, Liv, and her fiancé, Ian, and Robbie, all of us sitting in deadly silence as I stared at the meatloaf that dominated the middle of the table. My unease grew as Mom placed dishes of boiled potatoes and green beans beside the lump of baked meat.

If you didn't already know you were in trouble...

Rune leaned in his breath barely above a whisper. "You are *so* dead."

I barely resisted the urge to elbow my younger sibling. "Shut up. It could be they just want a healthy alternative."

"Meat loaf, Astrid? Really?"

Took her seat at the table reaching for her napkin.

Uh-oh. No bread rolls. I am about to be slaughtered.

"Please." She gestured at our surprise guest for the evening. "Robbie, do start."

The table winced collectively as he reached for the meatloaf, taking a hunk.

"Am I missing something?" he asked in a low tone as he passed the plate to me.

I bit my lip, shooting Mom a glance. She ignored me, serving Nan three plain potatoes.

This is it. This is how I die. Over a plate of meatloaf and unseasoned vegetables.

My mother was a former gourmet chef. Her worst dish was meatloaf because she didn't believe in cooking something that came out looking like a rather large poo.

I leaned toward Robbie, about to give him a heads up when my mother dropped a platter on the table with a clang, staring across the table at me.

"Really, Astrid? Really? You couldn't have

told us about this achievement? I had to hear about it from Martha Stanisbury who saw it on the news?"

I cringed at the hurt in her voice. "I'm sorry, Ma. But—"

"No buts," Dad interrupted, shaking his head. "You owe your family an apology."

My cheeks burned, my eyes beginning to sting. "I'm sorry for not telling you."

Are you going to admit why?

"Thank you for your apology," Mom said with a little sniff. "Now, why didn't you tell us before? Is this to do with your hair?"

I raised a hand, hovering it over my hair, a little part of me sighing in frustration.

I'd dyed my hair brown just before Thanksgiving. I'd been itchy, unsettled, and thought a new look might help. It hadn't but that didn't mean I didn't like the hair color.

"What's wrong with my hair?"

Mom waved me off. "That's not the true question here, Astrid. The question is why didn't you trust us?"

Because I'm a failure and didn't want to disappoint you.

The words stuck in my throat, shame swirling in my belly.

I sucked in a breath, the lie falling from my lips easily. "I didn't think it was that big a deal."

Mom pressed her lips together, her eyes flashing with annoyance. "And when it became a big deal?"

I looked at Robbie, my eyes pleading with him to help. He gave me an encouraging smile but didn't say anything, simply allowing me space to speak.

Ugh.

"I...." I swallowed, trying to conjure up a believable story.

A kernel of truth in a lie rings truer than a fabricated tale.

Thanks, Evil Astrid.

"I guess it was fear. And maybe a bit of doubt. Before Robbie read it and started tweeting, *Shadow Lies* was a certifiable flop. I guess I just thought... if I kept it to myself no one had to know it wasn't successful."

All head turned from me to watch Mom weigh my words.

"And your degree?"

Fuck.

I stiffened, casting my gaze around the table, finding my siblings all with their heads down, studiously shoveling meat into their mouths.

Thanks, team. I appreciate the support.

Though, in all fairness, I'd have done the same had I been in their shoes. And I had, many times before.

"I...." I choked, unable to push out the worlds.

"You?" Mom asked, raising an eyebrow in question.

"Failed."

There was a collective sucking in of breath, all heads lifting to stare at me.

My red face flushed hotter, humiliation churning my gut.

Failed. I'm a big fat failure.

"You.... Oh, Astrid." Any residual anger or hurt melted from my mother's face as she pushed to stand, immediately rounding the table. "Come here, my darling."

I shoved up, letting her pull me into a hug, savoring the feel of her arms around me, taking all the comfort she could give.

"You worked so hard," she whispered, her hand cupping my head. "I'm sorry, baby."

I swallowed, fighting the bitter tears that rose at her empathetic tone. "I'm sorry for failing."

"Did you do your best?"

I thought of all those nights working on my thesis, the extra study groups, the multiple meetings with my useless, sexist mentor.

We should have killed him with the stapler.

"Yes."

"Then you didn't fail. You just learned what

to do differently next time." She cupped my cheek, tilting my head down until she could press a kiss to my forehead. "Now, eat your dinner."

I watched her walk away, the table relaxing with Mom's blessing.

Not for long, Evil Astrid whispered. *It would have been easier if you'd laced the meatloaf with cyanide.*

I straightened my shoulders, determined to get this over and done with.

"Actually, I'm not going back."

The table froze, all heads whipping to me then across to Mom.

"Astrid?" She whispered her eyes wide. "What do you mean?"

"I'm not going back. I... I don't want to be an architect. I hate it. I've hated it for years but I didn't know what else to do. I thought I had to do... something. And it seemed as good as anything." My hands began to fly around as I tried to justify my decision. "I'm going to write novels. Don't worry, I'll pay you back for my schooling. Even if I have to—"

A thought occurred to me, an idea that might wipe the worried expression from my mother's face.

"Astrid?"

I looked at Robbie, the idea taking root,

giddy excitement beginning to bubble in my chest. "Robbie and I are going to co-write *Shadow Lies*."

"We're going to—" Robbie bit off, forcing a smile on his face. "Yep. That's exactly what we're doing."

"But you've never written a script before," Liv pointed out. "Either of you."

Robbie cleared this throat. "Actually, I have. It just wasn't very good. But *Shadow Lies* is already amazing. I expect it won't be too hard to work out how to translate it to the big screen."

I caught Dad's exasperated shake of his head.

"Dad, I'm sorry. But this is what I want to do. Even if it never gets made, *Shadow Lies* is selling well, thanks to Robbie."

"I wouldn't be surprised if it makes the bestseller lists this week," Rune commented as he forked a bland potato. "And Astie's self-published. More royalties for her. The book is also excellent. If she follows it up, she could make a lucrative career out of thriller novels."

My brother's praise which was so rarely delivered, felt doubly special as I knew he'd have read the book as soon as he found out about it.

"Thanks, bro."

He sent me a smile. "It's really good. Thank you for being an amazing author."

Erik slapped a hand on the table, drawing attention to him. "You'll need a lawyer. We're not having our sister get taken advantage of by some no-good actor."

Robbie flushed while Liv rolled her eyes.

"Ian?" She asked her fiancé, arching an eyebrow in his direction.

"I think I could handle it for ye." He said, swirling his wine gently in his glass. "But I'll be wanting a signed copy of ye book, Astrid. Or maybe two." He reached over, placing a large hand on Liv's gently rounding stomach. "We've got to support the tiny dictator once she arrives."

It was Erik's turn to roll his eyes. "As if you're hurting for money."

A trust fund child, Ian had more money than my entire family combined – not that you'd ever know it. The man looked like a sasquatch, all red hair and crazy beard. His fashion sense also left something to be desired, but he made my sister blissfully happy so I didn't mind.

Laura chuckled, pushing Erik's face away. "Well, I for one think this is an amazing opportunity, Astrid. Let us know what we can do to help. Will you need blood removal suggestions? Cause I once had to assist with cleaning a crime scene and—"

Laura, the Queen of Clean, was off, describing in gruesome but fascinating detail how to remove brain matter from fabric wallpaper as we continued to eat Mom's offering.

"All right," Nan tapped her fork against her plate, interrupting Laura's explanation. "As fascinating as splattered brain matter and cleaning agents are, let's change the subject before I decide I can't eat pie for dessert."

"Pie?" Liv asked, perking up. "What kind of pie?"

"Pecan," Dad said, serving himself a second helping of green beans. "And yes, *I* made it."

"Sune's a brilliant baker," Gabby told Robbie with a grin. "I'm trying to talk him into making our wedding cake."

"My son wants a book stack wedding cake. I'm not making that shit," Sune grunted, shaking his head.

"I said I'd accept a single book," Rune replied with a shrug.

"You!" Nan brought the attention back to her, her gaze narrowed in on Robbie. "Movie star, pick a subject."

Robbie threw me a wide-eyed glance.

"What would you like to talk about?"

Nan shrugged. "Anything *but* brain matter would be a good start."

"Er...." He cast a glance around the room, his gaze focusing on my chest.

Well, hello Mr. Huynh.

My body clenched, awareness spiking between us as he met my gaze.

"Movies!" He declared, turning away, a slight flush heating his cheeks. "Christmas movies. Which is your favorite and why?"

Excuse me? Christmas movies? He looks at my chest and thinks Christmas movies? Oh, this man is about to—

I silenced Evil Astrid.

"Christmas movies... hmm...." Nan nodded at my sweater. "Well, we all know Astrid's favorite."

I looked down, suddenly feeling like an idiot as I took in the *Home Alone* inspired ugly sweater.

He's a movie star you dolt. He's not going to be interested in some backwater failure of a woman.

And yet...

"Rune, you start," Nan directed.

"*A Christmas Carol.* Though I prefer the book."

The table collectively groaned, Erik throwing a bean in Rune's direction.

"Of course you do." Gabby patted her fiancé's hand.

"Sune?"

"*The Grinch*," Dad grunted. "There's something rather appealing about being alone for Christmas."

"Oh, hush." Mom laughed, slapping him lightly. "You all know mine."

Robbie shot me a raised eyebrow.

"*The Holiday*. Mom's a big romantic and loves a good Kate Winslet film."

"Well give me *Die Hard* any day," Nan declared raising her glass in a toast. "If I were forty years younger, I'd have married Bruce Willis and you'd all be movie royalty."

"If that's a Christmas movie then I'll eat my hat," Erik declared, wrapping an arm around Laura's chair and snuggling her into him.

"Oh yeah? Then what's yours?" Laura asked him.

"*Love Actually*. Emma Thompson is a queen and every time I watch it, I want to dick punch Alan Rickman."

I chuckled, looking at Robbie.

"*Blinky Bill*. It's an Australian cartoon about a koala. There's a whole series but every year they'd trot out the Christmas special. While my parents were celebrating with friends that's the movie I'd be in my bedroom watching."

"Just you?"

He laughed, nodding. "My parents had me late in life. A little surprise for both of them, I'm afraid. Their friendship group weren't exactly kid-people, and those who had children, the kids were already grown by the time I came along."

My heart squeezed at the thought of this lonely little boy watching Christmas movies by himself.

"Well, mine is *Rudolph*," Gabby declared, bopping Rune on the rose. "I love an underdog story."

"You know, I always thought he could do better." I shrugged. "Just seemed like those so-called friends were royal dicks."

Beside me, Robbie sniggered as the table groaned.

"Thanks for ruining Gabby's Christmas," Gabby said with a laugh, flicking me the bird.

"Any time."

"What's yours then?" Robbie asked. "Is it *Home Alone*?"

"Contrary to popular belief, it's actually not. Mine's the same as Ian, after all, he introduced me to it two years ago."

Eyebrows collectively raised around the table.

"*Arthur Christmas*," he said with a grin. "The grandfather cracks me up every time."

Liv rolled her eyes. "I should have known. You watched it three times last week."

"It's a good thing ye love me."

"Aye," she said in a terrible accent. "That it is."

They kissed as Mom stood. "Dessert! And a movie, I should think. How about *The Holiday*?"

With laughter we separated, clearing the table as pie was served, and coffee and tea handed out.

Liv caught me, gesturing to Robbie to follow, leading us into Dad's study.

She settled behind the desk, a giant slice of pie in front of her. She lifted her steaming cup of tea to her lips, blowing on it gently.

"This seems a bit redundant now, what with Astrid's dinner declaration. But go on, Robbie. Pitch your vision to us."

I settled on the settee, sipping my own tea as he turned away from us, offering his back. His shoulders hunched for a moment as if he were folding in on himself, then he sucked in an audible breath, straightened them, and spun back around his gaze terrifyingly blank.

"I decided to kill Ms. Avery on Tuesday at four o'clock."

Chills raced down my spine, goosebumps

dimpling my skin, the hairs on the back of my neck rising at his tone. He'd done something to his voice, it was lower, softer but so clear and horrifyingly devoid of inflection that you simultaneously revolted against him and inched closer to hear every horrific word utter from between his lips.

I lost myself in his monologue, his dead-eyed stare so perfectly capturing James that I could no longer conjure the image of the character I'd created. Now, there was only Robbie.

I've never been more attracted to someone in my life.

A phone rang, startling Liv and me. From his pocket, Robbie pulled the phone free, his blank expression still in place.

He slid his thumb across the face of the screen, his expression morphing into a charming mask that slid over his features with far too much ease.

"Ms. Avery? Yes, this is James. I've consulted my calendar, how does Tuesday at four sound?"

The switch from dead-eyed killer to charming guy-next-door was so abrupt, so jarring that Liv and I exchanged startled glances, our eyes wide and filled with questions.

He drew us back as he chattered with the fake caller, his expression animated up to the point he hit end, then the mask fell away, leaving death in its wake.

Perfection. He is utter perfection.

He lifted his head, his gaze meeting mine.

"I find I love the way they die."

He turned away from us, his body curving back into himself before he shook off the character, turning back around.

"Co-star?" Liv barked.

"Beatrix Bennett for Piper. The rest we'll need to audition for."

"Director?"

"Samuel Archer."

Liv nodded in approval. "Budget?"

"Twenty-five million."

"So low?"

He shrugged. "If we do it right, sure. This isn't a flash-bang blockbuster. This is quietly insidious. It's about the actors and the score. The cinematography. There are no explosions or car chases. Just a predator manipulating those around him."

Liv considered him for a moment as my stomach clenched at the casual way they discussed millions of dollars as if it were but a drop in an ever-expanding ocean.

"Alright. That makes sense to me, but we'll need a buffer of thirty-percent." She glanced my way. "Astrid?"

I swallowed, my heart hammering loud enough to drown out the television outside. "Yes?"

She arched an eyebrow, tilting her head in Robbie's direction. "It's your story, sis. You get to decide if he's going to bring this to life."

I looked at Robbie, his expression hopefully.

"I accept. On one condition."

"Anything."

"I want to write it. I want full creative control of the script, Robbie. I need to be involved in every aspect of its development."

He hesitated, glancing at Liv.

Please. I need this.

She sipped her tea, letting us work out the details.

"That's my one condition. Take it or leave it." I pressed my palms together in my lap, hating how damp they felt.

He nodded once then held out a hand, waiting for me to take it. I covertly wiped mine on my jean leg then took his hand, accepting a brisk shake.

"Let's make a movie."

CHAPTER 7

Robbie

This was a huge mistake.

I watched Astrid stare at the blank whiteboard, the marker turning over and over in her hand as she worried her lip, a frown marring her forehead.

We'd been at this for forty-minutes and no one work has been written, not one scene discussed. She'd arrived at the doorstep of my rental at the crack of dawn, whiteboard tucked under one arm, a bag overflowing with props and stationery thrown over the other.

I'd welcomed her into the condo with a smile, offering coffee and pastries. She'd accepted the coffee, waving off the breakfast sweets in order to get started.

Only, we'd hit a block. And that block was named Astrid Larsson.

At least she's a cute block. Would it be weird to tell her that?

She wore a red Christmas sweater today, the fabric so plush and soft that I wanted to reach out and compare its feel to that of Astrid's skin.

Wait. You want to what?

I frowned into my cooling coffee.

You're not into Astrid. You can't be. You're work colleagues now. Remember?

Besides, I'd been on a celibacy pledge for close to ten years, ever since I'd started getting decent parts. I didn't have time for romance, and hook-ups had never been my style.

And yet....

I shoved any thoughts of romance aside, downing the dregs of my cold coffee with a grimace.

"Okay, let's talk. What's the issue, Astrid?"

She glanced at me, a slight blush dusting her cheeks. "You'll laugh if I tell you."

I raised an eyebrow. "Try me."

She hesitated then handed me the whiteboard marker, digging through her prop bag to pull out a set of reindeer antlers.

"I need to wear these."

Don't laugh. Don't laugh. Don't laugh.

I nodded, swallowing my amusement and

forcing what I hoped was a blank expression on my face. "Okay, sure. I've seen weirder things than that. Whatever you need."

She blew out a breath, a small grin beginning to tug at her lips. "You think I'm weird."

"No more... eccentric maybe? I mean you write gruesome thrillers and yet look like a kindergarten teacher. It's an amusing dichotomy."

"Great," she laughed, rolling her eyes as she settled the antlers on her head. "I'm weird."

I opened my mouth to defend eccentricity but hesitated, aware of the risk of revealing too much of myself. I'd long ago learnt that people often took that information and sold it to the highest bidder.

You have to trust someone.

I swallowed, decided to take a chance.

"When I first started in the industry, I wore fake glasses."

Astrid laughed, her eyes twinkling. "Are you serious?"

"Completely." I leaned in, lowering my voice. "You can't tell anyone because I just brushed it off later as having reading glasses. But sometimes, when I'm particularly nervous about an audition or attending a gala or interview or whatever, I'll dig them out and wear them around."

"You didn't wear them yesterday."

I grinned, pushed up from the table, and went to the coat rack by the door. For a moment I dug through the pockets of my jacket before pulling the glasses free. I held them up, enjoying Astrid's surprised giggles.

"See? Even just having them on me is comforting."

She shook her head, the antlers swaying with the movement. "Why glasses?"

I shrugged, replacing them back into the pocket. "I don't know. Superman complex maybe? There's just something really reassuring about them. It's like I'm able to turn into someone else when I wear them. As if I'm marketing 'Robbie Huynh, Astipia's sweetheart', and not Robert Huynh, the guy they called Bob back at school."

"Bob?" Her eyebrows flew up.

I nodded, chuckling. "When I signed on with Catch 22 Productions, they made me change it. Said it didn't feel sexy enough."

Astrid wrinkled her nose. "They made you change your—" she cut herself off, her eyes losing focus for a moment.

"Uh, Astrid?"

"Shh." She held up a hand, staring off into

the distance for a moment. "Marketing.... You said you turned into someone else and it was all just marketing."

She pushed to her feet, urgently popping the cap on a whiteboard marker as she began to scribble in the top left-hand corner.

Opening scene – James at a pitch meeting. He's charismatic, charming, and likable.

"Oh," I whispered, leaning closer to catch her small murmurs as she wrote on the board. "I like that."

"He's going to be in marketing in the movie. We can't have the slow build-up as we did in the book, it's a different medium. And we don't want them to learn he's a serial killer just yet. We want them to like him. To feel for him. To be cheering him on."

"Unreliable narrator. I love it." I stood, reaching for my own marker and beginning to draw opposite Astrid on the board. "Let me storyboard this."

While Astrid wrote dot points for each of the scenes, I began to draw, building a set sketch.

"What if we don't know he's the killer until half-way? Like we build him up to be the hero, never showing the killer's face until there's a subtle reveal?"

"Ohh, that's evil." I lifted a hand for her to slap. "That's worthy of a coveted high-five."

She laughed, slapping my palm then turning back to make a note on the timeline she'd begun to build out. "This is surprisingly more fun than I anticipated."

I reached out, flicking her antler ears gently. "I'd say these certainly helped."

We got back to it, working out how her already incredible story could be adapted to the screen.

Matt wandered in a while later, scratching his chest. "Hey, you guys want some lunch? I was thinking about going and getting a sandwich from that café you like, Robbie."

I blinked, glancing up at the clock, startled to see that four hours had passed since we'd started.

"Um, yeah, that'd be great. Astrid?"

"Hm?" she was staring at her computer screen, having finished at the whiteboard.

"Lunch?"

"Sure. A coke, please."

I shared a grin with Matt.

"Just grab us whatever is on special. You need cash?"

Matt shook his head, tapping his pocket. "I'm good. You cool to stay here?"

"Yep."

He shot me a thumbs up before heading out, leaving Astrid and me to our work.

I studied her as she frowned at her screen, viciously backspacing.

"You okay?" I asked, pushing my sketchbook aside.

Astrid came back to herself slowly, blinking a few times as she disconnected from the laptop.

"Sorry... did you say something?"

I grinned, rising from my seat. "Come on, let's go for a walk."

"Walk?" Astrid asked.

"Uh-huh."

I grabbed our coats then led her from the room toward the back of the house.

"Where are we going?"

"Not far."

I paused at the door, helping her into her coat. For a moment her body grazed up against mine, her silky hair brushing against the back of my hands.

Kiss her.

Astrid pulled away turning around to face me.

"Outside? It's freezing."

"Yeah, but we need to clear our heads. We can only flow for so long."

I pulled my own jacket on then opened the back doors leading Astrid out onto the deck.

"It's windy!" She yelled; her words snatched by the gale.

"It's perfect! Come on!" I clutched her hands, pulling her down the short staircase and onto the private beach.

"What are we doing?" Astrid yelled, her hair whipping wildly about her.

"Screaming!" I tipped my head back, raised our joined hands, and let out a belly-deep roar, all the tension draining from me.

Astrid laughed, squeezing my hands. "You're crazy."

"Give it a go. It works. Promise!"

She sent me a laughing look then tilted her head back, closed her eyes, and let out a holler that would have made her Viking ancestors proud.

"Better?" I asked as she dropped our hands.

"Actually yeah."

Her cheeks were flushed, her nose beginning to redden, but her grin reached her eyes, their twinkle igniting an answering spark in me.

I grinned. "Again?"

"Let's do it."

With that, we tilted our heads back, raised

our hands, and screamed our stresses to the dark winter sky.

If only my overwhelming attraction could be so easily dispersed.

CHAPTER 8

Astrid

It had taken me less than three days to brush off any hero-worship I might have held for Robbie. Over the past two weeks, I'd come to learn that he was a funny, charming but absolutely human individual.

He didn't like when his pencils weren't sharp. He hated Jack cheese and green peppers (though he called them capsicum). He declared that his favorite movie ever was *The Princess Bride* and he'd fight anyone who called it a chick-flick. He loved dogs and felt neutral towards cats. He was allergic to papaya and loved to hum pop music under his breath when he concentrated.

And somehow, knowing all this made me

like him even more. These facts, these simple quirks that made up the complex being that was Robbie, had turned me from an admirer into a friend.

And yet you hope for more.

I sighed as I scanned yet another book into the system for yet another customer who was too frazzled by Christmas to be interested in maintaining a modicum of politeness.

I want to kiss the living daylights out of him.

I both love and hated that I wanted to kiss Robbie. He was a Good Guy (capitals included). He made me laugh, talked me through writers' block and had become a fixture at our family dinners. He helped Mom in the kitchen, chatted true crime podcasts with Nan, bemoaned politics with Dad, played with my nephews, teased Liv, discussed books with Rune, asked Gabby and Erik for sailing tips, and shared wine suggestions with Ian. He'd even met Gunnar and Ella via a video call. Ella—predictably—had flipped out.

It was as if he had been the missing piece in our jigsaw of a family. He fit. Perfectly.

And yet...

I wasn't sure if we had chemistry. Oh, sure, sometimes he'd look at me and there'd be a spark, a little flash of possibility.

And then it'd be gone. Vanishing so quickly I had to wonder if I imagined it.

"Here you go." I handed the bag to the customer offering him a smile. "Happy Holidays!"

He snatched the bag, ticking off something on his list before pivoting to leave, not even acknowledging my existence.

"Bah humbug," I muttered, rolling my eyes.

"I'd believe you if it weren't for that monstrosity of a cardigan."

I twisted, smiling in delight at Robbie. "What are you doing here?"

He pushed off the shelf he'd been leaning on, a coffee in each hand. "Waiting for you to be free. I wanted to run something past you."

He handed me the keep cup and I inhaled gratefully, enjoying the soothing scent of vanilla and rich dark blend.

"How did you know I'd need this? Are you a hero in disguise?"

He laughed, nodding. "Yep, call me Coffee Man. Here to deliver beans to those in need."

I couldn't help but appreciate his smile, his easy laugh, and his good humor.

God, just kill him already. Anything is better than this weird purgatory between love, lust, and the friendzone.

I shushed Evil Astrid, taking a long sip.

"So about tonight. I was thinking we could storyboard—"

I groaned, pressing a hand to my face and shaking my head. "Robbie, no. Not tonight. I'm wrecked. It's two days before Christmas. I need a break."

"Well... okay. What did you have in mind?"

I peeked at him from between my fingers. "You want to hang out with me?"

He frowned. "Sure. I mean, only if you want me to. I guess Matt and I could organize a movie or—"

"No!" I yelped, leaning forward to squeeze his bicep.

Jesus. He is built!

I cleared my throat. "Let's go to the Christmas markets. I can get some last-minute Christmas gifts, we can watch the tree lighting, listen to carolers, and eat like kings."

His lips curled into a half-smile. "I guess I could do that."

"Guess?" I tilted my head to the side. "Can't muster any excitement?"

"Oh, I'd say I'm pretty thrilled to be spending time with my girlfriend."

I froze, then laughed, forcing myself to relax even as a little pang of hurt speared my insides. "Ah yes, the old girlfriend schtick. We should really kill that before someone thinks we mean it for real."

Robbie watched me for a moment his gaze turning thoughtful. "Astrid, what if—"

"Excuse me? Do you work here?"

I sighed, stepping back from Robbie and turning to the waiting customer. "I do. How can I help?"

Out of the corner of my eye, I caught Robbie watching me, a strange expression on his face.

Seriously. Just kill him. The man is obviously clueless and we don't need that kind of negativity in our life.

I took another sip of coffee then put him from my mind, focusing entirely on the customer and their search for the perfect book.

"Okay, I concede," Robbie said, laughing as he took a bite of flammkuchen. "This is delicious."

"I told you!" I bumped my hip into his, grinning as I lifted my own slice of the delightful flatbread pizza-not-pizza to my lips. "Best part of Christmas is the food."

"Hor-ry schit!" Robbie yelped around a mouthful of meat and cheese. "Cuprul gumpers!"

I choked on my bite, snorting as I tried to swallow. "What did you say?"

Robbie caught my hand, dragging me across the square. "Couples jumpers!"

Jumpers?

I caught sight of the ugly sweaters displayed in the stall, laughing. "Really?"

"Yep." He began to peruse the options on hand as he held the remaining flammkuchen out for me to take. "You want the last piece?"

"Sure." I chewed, amused by his clear delight as he pulled sweater after sweater free, considering it then discarding it with a sigh.

"What are you looking for?" I asked, discarding out rubbish in a nearby trash can.

"Something we can wear to Christmas with your family."

"What?"

He held up a sweater pursing his lips together in a ridiculously attractively pout before discarding it. "Your mum invited me."

I love the way he says Mom.

"I've never had a big family Christmas. She said to wear an ugly sweater so I figured I should embrace a couple sweater theme." He glanced my way looking pointedly at my sweater which read *I'm sexy and I snow it* with a snowman waving.

I giggled, coming up beside him to begin

flicking through the rack. "Oh, what about this set?"

The two sweaters read, *I'm naughty* and *I'm nice*, each in either green or red.

"Nope, not special enough." He pulled a shirt combo free holding it out to me. "Thoughts?"

"Star Wars Christmas? Amateur. We can totally do better."

We both turned back to the rack, our hands brushing as we reached for the same sweater set. For a moment our gaze caught, our hands hovering in place, the heat from his skin warming mine.

Behind us Matt coughed, breaking the moment. With an awkward shift I moved back, giving Robbie space.

"What on earth...?" Robbie pulled the sweater free and we both erupted into laughter, catching each other's eye and laughing harder.

As we settled down, Robbie glanced Matt's way. "There're three options here. Do you think...?"

I doubling over my laughter returning with a vengeance as tears streamed down my face. "Oh my God, yes! A hundred percent yes!"

The stall owner, sensing a sale, rushed over. "We can personalize them in less than thirty minutes."

"Sold!" Robbie declared, reaching for his wallet. "One of these two, and this one with both on it, please." He nodded towards Matt who stood outside the stall watching the crowded marketplace closely. "The extra one is for him."

"I just need your sizes and a photo of your face and I'll have it all ready in a short while."

We took each other's photo, giggling so hard that we barely managed to take the image.

"He's going to hate you," I commented as we stumbled out of the stall and down the street.

"Oh, I know." Robbie rubbed his hands together gleefully. "I can't wait."

My sweater featured an elf with Robbie's face hanging a stocking above a fireplace framed by the words, *Well Hung*. Robbie's shirt was likewise Mrs. Claus pole dancing around a candy cane with my face with the words, *Santa's Favorite Ho*.

Matt's shirt featured both our faces dressed as Christmas elves hugging each other and the words *When I think about you, I touch my elf*.

Honestly, the best!

"Should we get some cider while we wait?" Robbie asked, glancing around.

"No, let's go ice skating." I shot him a grin. "You *do* ice skate, right?"

He shook his head. "Nope. But I'll give it a try."

We hired skates, Matt declining to join us.

"You kids have fun. I'll be fine here with my unbruised ass and hot cider."

"Grinch!" I teased, lacing up my skate. "Ready?"

Robbie wobbled awkwardly as he followed me the few steps across to the ice rink.

"It's simple. Just push and glide!" I threw my arms out, gliding across the ice.

"Simple, sure." He muttered, death gripping the sideboard.

"Come on." I held out my hands, wiggling my fingers with a cheeky grin. "I won't let you fall."

"Promises, promises, Astie. And to think I was going to buy you pie."

My heart skipped at the use of my nickname; the flash of desire now as familiar to me as his smile.

"Pie?"

"Mm, you said it was the quickest way to a Larsson woman's heart."

For a moment we stared at each other, something strange and exciting shimmering between us.

"So I did," I murmured, wanting to prolong the moment.

With a deep breath, Robbie let go of the sideboard, pushing away to wobble his way across to me.

I laughed at his awkward attempt, capturing his hand and holding him steady. "Just hold on to me, I'll pull you around while you get a feel for it."

I'd skated for years, playing hockey during winter. I'd been the woman's league's top goalie three years in a row. The ice rink didn't scare me.

Robbie death gripped me, his face a wreath of frown lines as he watched my feet slide across the ice.

"I think I got it," he murmured as we rounded the rink a second time.

"Alright, ready? On three. One... two...." I let him go, watching as he pushed his skate against the ice, mimicking my movement. "That's it! Well—"

He slipped, falling heavily with a slap on the ice.

"—done." I winced in sympathy. "Oh, dear." I couldn't stop the giggles as I skated to his side, assisting him to get up.

He winced, leaning heavily on me. "This is harder than the time I had to learn Romeo and Juliet in a week. Do you know how many freaking thou and dost that includes?"

I snorted, supporting him as he scrambled to his feet, his skates splaying to each side as he tried to brace himself. "Strong core, stand upright, find your balance, and then just... glide." I pushed off, lifting a leg and showing off a little as I glided away from him.

He watched, his face beginning to soften into an amused grin even as his hand were spread wide to steady his wobbly balance. "You can totally do one of those spinning things, can't you? Maybe a jump?"

"You mean like this?"

I picked up some speed racing down towards the empty end of the rink, I pushed off the ice leaping into a graceful arch before landing and immediately throwing myself into a fast twist. I finished with a flourish, one hand pointed down behind me, the other raised in the air above my head with a sassy flick of my fingers, shooting him a wink.

Robbie clapped and nearly slipped over again, laughing as his arms shot wide, his legs locking as he shook his head. "This was a terrible idea!"

"You wanted to do it!" I called as I skated back his way. Out of the corner of my eye I caught sight of a young group of girls staring at us, their gazes narrowed in on Robbie.

Uh-oh. Evil Astrid senses trouble.

Robbie shuffled across to the sideboard, one hand clinging to it as he tried to find his footing.

"I think you have a fan club," I said, tilting my head in the girls' direction.

Robbie slowly raised his head, glancing their way then swearing when they saw him look, their phones immediately coming out to snap pictures.

"Fuck. Astrid, sorry, but... we gotta go."

"What? Why?"

Matt appeared on the other side of the sideboard. "Robbie, we—"

"I saw. Let's motor."

"Wait. What's happening?"

Robbie quickly shuffled off the ice, Matt supporting him back to the bench where we'd stored our shoes.

"What's happening?" I asked as I plonked down on the bench beside him, beginning to unlace my boots. "What did I miss?"

"They're coming." Matt hissed; his gaze trained on the girls now hurrying around the rink. "Hurry!"

"Make sure Astrid's safe," Robbie barked, tugging on his boots. "You get me, Matt? They can't touch her."

"Are they fans?" I asked, utterly bewildered. "Why do we need to—"

"OH MY GOD! IT'S ROBBIE HUYNH!"

My head snapped up, my eyes widening as I saw the cluster of girls now scrambling through the crowd to get to us.

I managed to pull my boots on just as Matt hauled us both up, shoving us in the opposite direction to the oncoming cluster. The festive mood of the crowd shifted as people began to look our way, their eyes widening, their expressions turning into something like adoration mixed with selfish desire.

Shit. Was I like that the first time I met Robbie?

"Fuck. Go!" Matt hissed, shoving us deeper into the crowd. "Hurry."

We scrambled, pushing our way through the crowd and back into the main market.

"Robbie! Robbie!" The girl's screaming had drawn attention and as people registered that a world-famous movie star was in their midst, they turned rabid.

"Oh my God!"

"Wait! I want a selfie!"

Word spread faster than we could move, the crowd now snatching at him as we tried to leave.

Holy shit. This is how people die. This is how I could die. Oh my God!

I began to throw my elbows as Matt attempted to bodily plow us through the crowd, his expression deadly.

"We gotta get out of here!" Robbie yelled. "Astrid's gonna get hurt."

"You're gonna get fucking hurt," Matt barked, his gaze scanning for options. "There! Head for the toilets. We'll loop around the back and out to the main street."

I caught a flash of a blonde head towering far above the crowd.

"Wait! It's Rune!" I snatched Robbie's hand, pulling him along behind me, Matt swearing but following as we headed towards my giant of a brother "Rune! Wait! Rune!"

My brother, his arm slung snuggly around Gabby, her arm around his waist, turned to stare at us as we emerged from the crowd.

"Astie? What are you guys—"

"No time! Can we borrow your car?"

"Why—"

"There he is! Over there!" A shrill female voice squealed followed by a cacophony of screaming.

"Quick!" I bounced on my toes, panic, and no small amount of fear injecting adrenaline in my veins.

Rune fumbled in his pocket holding the keys out. "We're parked at the store."

"Go!" Matt bellowed behind us. "Run!"

Hand-in-hand Robbie and I sprinted through the market, dodging shoppers and couples, nearly taking out a family with triplets.

"They're gaining!" I panted, chancing a glance over my shoulder.

"Down here!" Robbie pulled me into a small alley, Matt at our back. We dashed down it, squeezing through the tiny gap between the buildings, my hand clasped tightly in Robbie's.

"Go!" Matt called. "I'll slow them!"

The alley spewed us out onto the main street, the crowds sparce compared to that at the market.

"Which way?" Robbie asked, glancing this way and that.

"Towards the store, this way!"

Hand-in-hand we sprinted down the street, rounding a corner and making a mad dash toward the safety of The Literary Academy.

As we got close, I spied Ashley, the assistant store manager, closing up.

"Ash!" I yelled, my lungs burning. "Ashley! Open it!"

She turned; her eyes wide as stared at us barreling down on her.

Without a word she stepped aside, holding the door open for us to rush through then closing it behind us with a click.

"You got keys?" She yelled through the thick door as she locked it from the other side.

"Yes," I replied, my voice sounding like an asthmatic wheeze more than a reply.

"Okay! You kids have a good night." We heard her move, her footsteps crunching on the gravel outside leaving us in the dark bookstore.

Robbie bent over, bracing his hands on his knees as he sucked in a breath. "Fuck."

I huffed out a laugh, bracing my hands on my hips and tipping my head back to suck in air. "What the fuck, Robbie?"

"I know."

He groaned, pushing to a stand, somehow his breathing settling into a normal rhythm. The man didn't even look sweaty. Bastard.

"It's unfortunately not that uncommon."

"We lost Matt."

He huffed out a laugh. "You might have missed it, but the man sacrificed himself for us. He likely bodily blocked those girls at the alley to allow us time to get away."

I shook my head. "Your life is insane."

"I know."

His phone chirped and he pulled it out checking the message.

"Matt's safe. Said to stay put. The girls are roaming the streets. He'll come by in an hour or so when it's all clear."

I shivered, wrapping arms around myself.

"What do you think they'd have done if they got you?"

He shrugged off his coat, tossing it over a chair then rolled back the arm of one sleeve baring his bicep.

Oh Lordy, I'm turning into a desperado. Has a bicep ever invoked such lust? I feel like I should be bearing an ankle in return. Shit, am I in a period drama?

He raised a finger tapping a faint scar on his bicep. "Last year I got caught in an airport toilet." He dropped his hands reaching for his shirt and lifting it to just below his nipples. He twisted slightly, showing me a thick welt on his right side.

"Three months ago, I tried to see a movie like a normal person. Big mistake. I lost two fistfuls of hair and ended the night with three stitches."

Unbidden, my hand lifted, my fingers reaching out to trail just below the healing skin.

Robbie sucked in a breath stilling under my hand.

For a moment neither of us spoke, just watched as my fingers moved across his dark skin.

"Astrid...." My name sounded like a plea on his lips.

I raised my head, my eyes meeting his. Our

gazes clashed, desire erupting between us. Our bodies shifted and in less than a heartbeat he had me clasped to him, his hands fisted in my hair, his mouth a breath from mine.

"Astrid... I...."

I pressed forward unable to stand being separate from him. I needed his taste on my lips and his breath in my lungs.

I needed him.

Moisture pooled between my legs, my body instinctively responding to his.

He murmured my name then bent, boosting me up and stepping forward until my back hit the bookshelf behind me.

Oh, this boy is trouble.

CHAPTER 9

Robbie

I'd wanted Astrid since the moment I'd seen her all those weeks ago at Thanksgiving. I could admit that now as I tasted her mouth, committing this moment to memory.

I forced myself to pull back, my hands to drop to the edge of her sweater.

"Can I....?"

She nodded, her lips swollen from our kiss, her eyes glazed with desire. My cock throbbed, desperate to feel her wet heat around me.

I pushed her coat off letting it pool on the ground. With deliberate slowness I tortured us both, gently lifting her cardigan to reveal soft creamy skin. Up and up, I pulled the material, her arms raising to allow me to pull it off and toss it aside. Before I'd even fully removed it, my lips found hers, desperate for another taste. Another kiss. Another stolen moment.

Perfection.

With a groan I pulled back, taking her in. Her full breasts were encased in black lace, her abundant curves making my mouth water as she kicked her boots off.

I ripped my shirt free then dropped my hands to her fly, fumbling with the zipper as her hands reached out to clasp my hips, holding us steady.

"You okay?" I whispered as I began to push her jeans down, wiggling the material over her hips and thighs, crouching to pull it down her legs and clear of her feet.

"Oh, I'm getting there."

I chuckled, the sound like gravel as I sucked in a breath, catching her scent.

God have mercy.

I slipped her jeans free, cupping her socked feet, smiling at the reindeer faces on the toes. "You want these on or off?"

"On. I don't want to kill you with my cold feet."

I grinned, sliding fingers slowly up her legs until I found the bottom of her boyleg underwear. "What about these?"

She bit her lip, her body flushed with desire. "Off."

Heat sizzled my blood as my fingers turned clumsy, fumbling with the material. I finally tugged her underwear free, the material gratifyingly soaked with her need.

Astrid stepped free and I brought the fabric to my face breathing deep.

"Robbie what—"

I caught her startled gaze, knowing mine was fierce. "You smell divine."

She shuddered, her hips undulating towards me.

I lifted up to press kisses across her hip bones, pausing above her mound, her curls tickling my chin. "You okay if I taste you?"

"You going to ask me every time you want to touch me?" She asked, her eyelids closed, her head tipped back as a cute smile touched her lips.

"Consent is sexy."

"Mm... well, I consent to anything and everything you want to do."

Thank God.

I dipped my head, my fingers parting her, revealing her tender flesh to my gaze.

"Fucking gorgeous."

I leaned in, breathing over the sensitive skin, grinning when her hands dropped to my shoulders, her nails leaving crescent shaped marks in my flesh.

I flicked out my tongue, closing my eyes as I savored the first glorious taste of her.

"Fucking fuck, Astie. You taste fucking amazing."

"Don't stop," she cried, her hands fisting my hair to pull me back to her. "Keep going!"

"Stop?" I chuckled, allowing her to press me back to her core. "Never."

Not even a million orcs could distract me from this moment.

I teased her with tongue and lips, carefully grazing my teeth across her sensitive skin, loving her breathy moans and startled gasps.

I dropped one hand, unzipping my jeans and shoving them down my hips far enough to pull my cock free, fisting myself roughly as I ate Astrid out.

I focused in on her clit, learning what made her sigh and whimper, what had her clenching and clutching at me, her sweet begging sending my own need soaring.

I found a rhythm, my tongue worshipping her clit. I lifted my spare hand to press a finger against her, filling her greedy body.

With a cry, Astrid arched riding my face with wild abandoned. No longer in control, I gave over, loving how she used me to reach for her pleasure, loving how she came in a hot, wet clench of lusty need.

"Robbie!"

I grinned, surging to my feet, immediately unbuckling her bra, replacing the cups with my hands.

"You come so prettily, Astie." I leaned down to blow air across her nipples. "Could you come just from me playing with these pretty breasts?"

She whimpered, her eyes wide as she watched me close the gap, my mouth suckling. My shaft pressed against her, trapped in the cradle of her thighs, throbbing with the need to fill her.

Patience.

I lifted my head, replacing my tongue with my fingers as I turned to her other breast, giving it the same dedicated attention.

Her head fell back against the bookshelf, books falling around us.

"I want to taste you," she murmured her hips grinding against me. "Please, Robbie."

"Mm?" I lifted my head, capturing her lips, my tongue tangling with hers.

We kissed, hard and desperate, my thumbs raking over her nipples as we ravished each other's mouth.

Don't come. Don't come. Don't fucking come.

I pulled her into my arms, hauling us across

the space and down into the maze of bookshelves, the dark of the store enveloping us.

"Robbie!"

I found a small study nook, complete with a desk.

Perfect.

With one last stagger, I stumbled us across to the desk, boosting Astrid onto it and positioning her until I was cradled between her legs, her breasts pressed deliciously against me.

She leaned in, her teeth nipping at my collar bone and I cursed, shoving at my jeans, my cock jutting proudly from above the fly.

She shifted, licking her way down to my nipples, nipping at the sensitive flesh, a hard groan ripping from my throat.

"You little minx." I fisted her hair, tilting her head back to ravish her mouth. She squirmed against me, her hands snaking between us to clasp my cock.

Danger, Will Robinson, danger!

I continued to kiss her, loathed to pull back as her fingers curled around my thick erection, her hands pumping my cock slow and tight, precum beading at the tip. Her thumb flicked out, capturing the moisture and using it to ease her glide.

My body arched closer, my cock throbbing at her ministrations.

I reached down, capturing her hand, pulling back just enough to caution her.

"Not yet. Keep going and it'll be over far too soon."

Her eyes flashed but she withdrew her hand. With deliberate provocation, she drew her fingers to her lips, licking away any remaining precum.

Holy fucking Christ. This woman is....

I swore, pulling her back into me, forcing my tongue between her lips, fucking her mouth.

A strangled moan escaped Astrid and I swallowed it, letting it feed me.

"Your fucking mouth," I whispered, beginning to pepper kisses along her cheeks, down her throat, across her collarbone.

I love this woman. Fuck, I love her.

The revelation didn't startle me. The feeling had been building for weeks. Oh, I knew it was far too soon. Knew people would say it couldn't possibly be love.

But I knew the truth. Deep in my soul, the knowledge took root, immediately flowering.

Astrid was everything I'd ever wanted. Cheeky and kind. Fun and serious. Desirable and delightful. I wanted to spend every moment with her. Every part of her fit every part of me.

I love her.

"Robbie...." Her needy little moan set me off.

I fisted my cock, guiding it to her core, arching back slightly to watch as the head of my cock bridged her sex, beginning to stretch her as I eased inside.

"Oh, God. Oh, fuck. Oh, my fucking God!"

Her cries fueled the fire in me, her liquid heat and tight, clutching pussy now defined paradise.

I thrust, my eyes practically rolling back in my head as her muscles stretched, working to accommodate my width. I may not have been the longest guy in the world, but I had most beat on thickness.

"So big, so big, so big," Astrid's chant had me chuckling.

"Just for you," I whispered against the shell of her ear. "You okay there, Astie?"

"I...." her voice lost power while her hands roamed my skin as if unsure of where to land.

"Hold on, minx. I got you."

She linked her arms around my neck, and arched her hips, a gasp tearing free as I fed her more of my cock.

"That's it. Take me, Astie."

I stroked deeper inside her, groaning as her body clutched at my cock.

"More, more, more, more!"

"More? Such a greedy girl," I praised.

I pulled back then thrust in hard, loving how her body bowed against me, her head falling back, her sweet little cunt holding me tight.

Reality fell away, any memory of the close shave from early disappeared as I gave myself over to Astrid.

I want to brand her. Mark her. Prove to the world that she's mine.

My cock throbbed, my balls drawing up as my climax began to bear down on me.

Don't come. Don't come. Don't come.

Astrid screamed, her body breaking, her little cunt spasming as her orgasm shattered her into a million pieces.

Yes!

I erupted, fucking her into the desk, my cock pounding into her clutching flesh.

I had a mind to pull out a fraction before I came, cum coating her curvy belly and generous tits.

Fuck yes!

Without thinking, giving in to some mindless, primal instinct, I scoped a finger of cum then reached down, rubbing it against her clit, playing with her sensitive flesh.

"Robbie!"

With a dark huff, I continued to stroke her body until Astrid came in a screaming, begging, panting wet mess, collapsing back on the desk, her hand reaching down to still my fingers.

"Good?" I asked, pressing light kisses to her skin.

"I think you killed me."

I chuckled, the raging desire subsiding. "But what a way to die, hm?"

She opened one eyelid giving me a droll glare. "That's not going in the script."

"Oh, I never doubted it."

We smiled our passion cooling, our bodies completely sated. I found this, this moment where I took care of her and we giggled and cuddled after amazing sex, this is what I wanted for the rest of my life.

Sex was great but Astrid? She was what made each moment magnificent. I'd forever choose this woman above all others.

Thank God you don't have to choose.

I opened my mouth, about to declare my undying love when she snapped up to a seat, her eyes wide.

"Oh no! Robbie! Our sweaters!"

I chuckled, rolling my eyes and she pushed past me, scrambling for her clothes.

"I see ugly sweaters get more attention than me."

She rolled her eyes, pulling on her bra. "You did great. I am thoroughly, and I mean this, satisfied. But ugly Christmas sweaters are a Larsson tradition. And it's your first Christmas with us. We *need* to get yours."

I paused one leg half in my jeans. "Sorry, did you say, *first* Christmas?"

She froze her arms in her sweater. "Um... is that too presumptuous?"

I dropped my jeans, closing the distance between us to cup her head, staring into her gorgeous eyes. "Presume away. I'm definitely not going anywhere. This?" I pressed into her. "You are too amazing by half. I'm not letting you get away."

She melted, her body sinking into mine, her hand coming up to lay over my heart.

"Robbie."

I bent, kissing her, loving the way my name tasted on her lips.

As Jerry McGuire said, she completes me.

CHAPTER 10

Astrid

I pulled the ribbon on the gift box tight, repositioning the tag until it sat just-so then slid it under the tree.

"Ready?" Mom asked, placing a plate of cookies on the coffee table.

"Yep."

She leaned over, brushing a stray hair from my cheek before sitting down beside me, leaning into my side. "Astie, I owe you an apology."

I started, my head swiveling to stare at my mother. "Sorry?"

She smiled, her expression melancholy. "You're my baby. Oh, not in age but we all know Rune was never a child. That boy came out a forty-year-old man. You though? You were my sweet baby girl, the one I never had to worry about—unlike your siblings."

She sighed, reaching out to cup my face. "And then you return from college a strange being. Secretive, changing your appearance, no longer my bright, shiny daughter. I worried." Her thumb grazed my cheek, a gentle smile touching her lips. "And now I see what happened. You tried to please us instead of following your own path. My beautiful girl, this life you're making? It's exactly who you were always meant to be. Brown hair or blonde, you are finally living. And it delights me that your shine is back."

Tears blurred my vision. "Ma...."

"I love you, my dearest Astrid. We're so proud of you."

She leaned forward pressing a kiss to my forehead.

"I love you, Ma."

She smiled. "Good. And now, tell me about your Robbie. Is it serious?"

I bit my lip, a flush heating my cheeks as I nodded.

"Mm, a mother always knows. Don't be afraid. If he makes you happy, don't wait."

"We've only known each other a short time."

"You know my feelings about time." She

squeezed my hand. "Your soul knows when it has found its other half. Don't question it. Embrace."

My parents had married less than three hours after meeting, they'd just known. And five kids, and nearly fifty years later they still had the most beautiful love.

I nodded, reaching out to wrap my arms around her, hugging her tight.

"Oh, sorry."

We both twisted from our seat on the carpet, catching sight of Robbie as he retreated from the room.

"Nonsense!" Ma called, stopping him with a wave. "Come in, come in!" She pushed up with a heavy groan, throwing me a laughing eye-roll. "These old bones ain't what they used to be."

As I pulled myself together, Ma greeted Robbie, patting him on the cheek and giving him a motherly hug.

"Go on in, our little Astie has something for you."

I watched him stroll across the lounge his body loose and relaxed, his chest clad in the sweater that matched mine.

I made love to that man last night. And the day before. And the day before that.

In fact, I'd made love to Robbie every day and night since we'd lost control on the desk in

The Literary Academy. Surrounded by books and quiet, that moment would forever be etched on my soul.

I love him. Completely. Crazily. Irrationally. I. Love. Him.

He eased down onto the carpet, crossing his legs and offering me a lopsided grin. "Well, hello, gorgeous." He leaned across, pressing a lingering kiss to my lips.

"Hey yourself." My stomach fluttered even as the pleasure of being in his space relaxed me. "I have something for you."

"Oh really? Is it a knife?"

I grinned, shooting him a wink. "Maybe. Open it."

"Uh-uh." He shook his head, shrugging a backpack off and pulling it around to unzip it. "You first."

From its depth, he withdrew a soft, flat package handing it over.

"Is this another sweater?" I laughed as I took the package.

"Open it and see."

I ripped into it finding two sweaters, both with the same writing. I lifted the soft fabric free of the wrapping, reading the cursive on the front.

Our First Christmas as Mr. and Mrs.

Under the writing were pictures of pies.

I stared at the fabric, desperately trying not put two and two together and come up with a marriage proposal.

"Sorry, what?"

He huffed out a nervous laugh. "You said pies were the way to a Larsson woman's heart so...." He cleared his throat, his gaze serious and intense. "Will you marry me, Astrid?"

I gapped at him, shock rendering me completely dumb. A moment of silence followed his declaration.

"It doesn't have to be today," he rushed to add, filling the silence I'd left. "Fuck. It's too soon, right? Shit. Look, it doesn't have to be a proposal or anything... I mean... unless you want it to be. That is to say... um... I just..." He ran a hand through his hair, the strands sticking up at odd angles.

"You just?" I asked, my heart in my throat, giddy joy unfurling.

"I just think you're wonderful, Astrid. Completely amazing. Honestly, you're everything. You delight me, frighten me, your mind is a freaking scary-wonderful place. I love listening to you laugh. I love holding you. I love kissing you. I love you. I know it's way too fast and this is completely irrational but—"

I threw myself at him, knocking us both backward and into the coffee table.

"Oof! What are you—"

I covered his mouth with mine putting all my passion and feeling into our kiss.

His mouth opened under mine, our tongues tangling, hands urgently tugging at each other's clothing.

"Yes!" I cried against him as I pulled back, rocking up to rip his sweater from his body. "A million times, yes!"

"Yes? What are you—Oh! Astrid! Robbie! What are you doing?" My mother's startled cry had us freezing, our heads twisting to stare at her in shock.

Oh, that's right. It's Christmas Day, you're at your parents' house, you just got engaged to a freaking movie star, and your mother just walked in on your trying to strip your fiancé naked.

Shit, I need a distraction!

"Robbie and I are getting married!" I squeaked.

My mother's face morphed from horrified to ecstatic in less than a heartbeat.

"Oh my God! He said yes!"

She surged forward dropping to her knees to wrap us both in a hug.

Under me, I could feel Robbie's thick erection immediately droop, the poor guy looked mortified as my mother practically strangled him.

"What's going on?" my father asked from the doorway.

"Sune! They're getting married!"

Robbie shot me a startled look and I laughed, leaning in to kiss him.

Behind us the family began celebrating as the news moved through the house, cries of delight coming from the kitchen and dining room.

"I love you."

"So, it's a definite yes?" he asked his adorable grin in place.

"Sure," I leaned back giving him a saucy wink. "But I look forward to seeing the terms of the contract first."

He threw back his head laughter spilling free.

My phone dinged and I pulled it free, laughing when I saw the notification for family chat.

LIV ADDED ROBBIE TO GROUP CHAT.

ELLA

Oh! I take it they're serious?

GUNNAR

Should someone warn him?

ERIK

Nah. He got the craziest one of
us all. I think he'll be fine.

I lifted the phone, snapping a selfie of us then sending it through. "Welcome to the family. You're official now."

He smiled, pressing his forehead against mine. "There's honestly nowhere I'd rather be."

It wasn't until later that night that I finally got to hand Robbie my gift.

With bated breath, I watched from the end of the bed as he untied the ribbon and lifted the lid on the box, the ribbon pooling over his chest giving me all sorts of naughty ideas.

"Astrid...." He lifted the bound screenplay free from the box, running a finger along the cover. "This is...."

"For you." I reached out, capturing his hand, tangling our fingers. "And for me. Writing this has given me the greatest pleasure of my life. This is the path I want to take. And I want to share it with you. Open it."

I let go of his hand watching as he opened the cover to the first page.

Dear Robbie,

How about we make this official?

Marry me!

Astrid

He looked up, his gaze electric.

"I know I'm late," I gave him a lopsided grin. "But it's nice to know we're on the same page."

He surged up, the screenplay forgotten as he wrapped arms around me, pushing me back down on the bed, his body covering mine. "I fucking love you."

"To quote Han Solo," I grinned, running my thumb across his lip. "I know."

And we spent the rest of the night consummating that love.

EPILOGUE ONE

Robbie

I looped an arm over Astrid's chair, gratified when she leaned into me, needing the reassurance only she could give me.

"Nervous?" She asked in a whisper.

"Fucking terrified," I admitted with a laugh, my spare hand digging into my jacket pocket to thumb the glasses tucked safely inside.

She cupped my cheek, pressing a kiss to my chin. "You've got this, Robert Huynh. This is your moment."

On the stage above us, the actress smiled prettily as the cameras zoomed in.

"These five actors have awarded moviegoers with truly magnificent stories. They touched our hearts, ravished our minds, and thrilled our souls. Tonight's nominees for best actor are," the famous actress paused for dramatic effect before rattling off the names of my fellow actors, leaving me to last.

Astrid's hand found mine, giving me a squeeze.

"And Robert Huynh, *Shadow Lies*."

The audience applauded as the highlight reel played, a hush fell over the crowd as it ended.

"And the Oscar goes to...." The actress opened the envelope. "Robert Huynh, *Shadow Lies!*"

Astrid shrieked, throwing herself on me, pressing a frantic kiss to my lips.

"Go!" She ordered, dropping back in her seat. "Go accept your award!"

In stunned disbelief I walked up the aisle, accepting handshakes and backslaps before hopping up the three stairs to the stage.

The actress shook my hand, kissing my cheek before handing me the award and stepping back.

I turned, seeing a standing ovation as cameras flashed and people shouted praise.

"Wow," I said into the microphone looking down at the award glittering in my hand. "Who would have thought it, hey? Winning an Oscar for killing people."

There was laughter and cheering from the audience.

I looked up, searching the crowd, finding Astrid. "There are so many people to thank for this amazing award. Firstly, thank you to the academy for this privilege."

I looked around, finding my agent, my director, and my producer in the crowd.

"To Liv Larsson-Campbell from Freya Productions, thanks for taking a chance on me and this script. I know it was a risk but I think we can both agree it paid off."

Liv laughed, blowing me a kiss, Ian standing proudly beside her.

"To Glenn, my agent, and his entire crew. Thank you for your support over the years. I wouldn't be here if you hadn't taken on a punk-ass kid from Australia."

Glenn grinned, shooting me a thumbs up.

"To all the cast and crew who worked on *Shadow Lies* this film wouldn't have been half as amazing without you. To Beatrix Bennett, my amazing colleague, and partner in crime, who brought this phenomenal story to life, and Samuel Archer, who took the script and our vision and directed the shit out of it, and to everyone who worked on *Shadow Lies*, this award is as much yours as it is mine."

Applause and more cheers. My costar giving a little bow in my direction.

"To everyone who has helped on this journey; my family, my friends, my teachers, and colleagues, and a million other people. Thank you for keeping me humble and lifting me up. For telling me that I could do this even when I thought it wasn't possible."

I sucked in a breath, meeting Astrid's gaze, smiling at the tears sliding unashamedly down her cheeks.

"And to the woman who made this all possible, Astrid Larsson, my gorgeous wife. Thank you for saying no a hundred-and-five times before finally trusting me with this story. It just made me work a hundred-and-six times harder to ensure this was the best movie it could be."

There was laughter at that, Astrid blowing me an air kiss. I held up the Oscar, holding it out towards her.

"This is yours, Astie. The script you wrote, the chance you took, the love and terror you built into each and every scene, you are phenomenal, you are brilliant, and you terrify me and delight me each and every day. We said dream big, we said we were aiming for the best, we said we wanted nothing but perfection." I placed one hand over my heart. "Well, we did it, Astie. *You* did it. I love you," I paused dramatically. "And I just want everyone watching to know that if I ever go missing don't bother looking—my wife knows how to hide a body."

Another round of laughter and applause as I looked back at the audience. "Thank you, and good night."

I stepped away from the podium, following the ushers as they lead me from the stage.

"Can someone get my wife, please? I want to share this with her."

One of them scurried off as they took me through to the green room, a makeup artist hurrying over to do a final touch up before I headed into the press area.

Questions were thrown thick and fast, cameras popping until all I could see were squiggles of light.

Questions done, my publicist ushered me through to a small room where Astrid stood waiting, her own Oscar clutched in her hand.

"You won!" She squealed, throwing herself at me.

"I can't believe it. *Shadow Lies* is cleaning up."

"We have to hurry; they're announcing Best Motion Picture."

We scurried outside, thankful for the slight break in commercial filming.

Shadow Lies had won multiple awards prior to tonight, raking in BAFTAs, Golden Globes, and Film Critic awards.

It'd rocked the box office, cashing in staggering figures its first weekend and every weekend after. We were a runaway hit, and Astrid deserved every piece of praise.

We hurried to our seats, accepting congratulations along the way, shooting friends and family air high-fives and kisses across the room.

"And the nominees are...."

I gripped her hand, clutching Astrid close.

"It's okay, we're still amazing even if we don't win," Astrid whispered, her fingers squeezing mine. "I'll still love you tomorrow."

I chuckled, pressing a kiss to her temple. "But perhaps a little less?"

She grinned, teasing me. "Only a fraction. But there's always next time."

Our attention was drawn back to the stage.

"And the Oscar goes to...."

EPILOGUE TWO

Astrid

I pushed back from my desk, tossing the antlers next to my laptop and standing with a groan, my hands immediately dropping to press into my lower back.

"Hey, you okay?"

Robbie's hands gently brushed my own away, his thumbs digging into the tight muscles of my lower back as he massaged the muscles. He pushed me forward slowly until I was bent at my hips, my hands braced on the desk, giving him ready access to my back.

"Mm, I am now," I muttered.

He chuckled, leaning forward to press a kiss to my neck as his fingers continued to work my tight muscles.

"It's done," I said, my eyes drifting closed as I turned into putty under his hands. "Needs some spit and polish but it's done."

His fingers halted, his body freezing. "What?"

I twisted my neck, looking at him over my shoulder. "*Turn Around*. It's done. You want to read it?"

He swallowed; I could see the indecision on his face.

With a soft huff of amusement, I pushed away from the desk, patting him on the shoulder. "Go on. I'll have a nap while you read."

"I love you!" He called as he took my abandoned seat.

"Oh, I know. That's why you're totally taking me out for dinner tonight."

"Your wish, my command."

I woke hours later, feeling refreshed and less like a woman on a deadline.

I stepped into the shower, determined to remove myself of the swamp monster feel on my skin. Robbie entered his naked body immediately embraced by the steam and water.

"Mm, hello," I whispered, my hands coming up to run over his muscular chest. "I didn't think you'd be joining me, Mr. Huynh."

"Well, Mrs. Larsson- Huynh, it appears that

I'm in the mood for some nookie." He nuzzled my neck, his lips grazing the sensitive skin. "And I just finished."

I braced, ready to take on his feedback. "Go on then, what did you think?"

"Three words – Best Motion Picture."

I laughed, tossing my wet hair away. "You're still chasing that award?"

"Mm, you deserve a clean sweep, Astie. You were robbed last time. Best Screenplay, Best Actor, you deserved to get Best Motion Picture. This movie? It's gonna be the one to take them all, Best Actress, Best Screenplay, all of them. I can feel it."

His hands drifted down, cupping my gently rounding stomach. "But we'll wait till after this one comes."

I laughed, leaning against him, letting Robbie hold me as water ran over our skin, heating us. "Do you ever worry that he'll be some kind of psychopath? What with you being an actor and me having the brain of a serial killer?"

"She." He corrected, both of us still locked in a battle of wills. "And babe, you wear holiday-themed underwear year-round. Last Christmas you dressed as an elf for three days. Our daughter never had a chance."

With that, he kissed me, deliciously, toe-curlingly, deep and slow.

"Mm," he murmured against my lips. "Love you, Astie."

"Love you too, Robbie."

"Bed or desk?"

"Both?"

He chuckled, his hands running down my back to cup my ass. "Perfect."

Thank you so much for reading The Christmas Contract! I hope you adored Astrid and Robbie!

Desperate for more Astrid and Robbie?
Check out the bonus chapter on my website
EvieMitchell.com

You can find the rest of the Larsson Siblings and some bonus extra Larsson's as well as other books on my website at
www.EvieMitchell.com

Get 10% off your next purchase via my website by using the code EBOOK10

ABOUT THE AUTHOR

Hey, I'm Evie Mitchell.
I'm a thirty-something romance author (she/her/hers) living with disability. I believe in inclusion, accessibility, and fierce romance. My loves include steamy romance novels, my sexy husband, our THREE sausage dogs (THE FUR!!!), and my ever-growing collection of book-related mugs.

As a woman with a diverse work history, including in areas such as hospitality, retail, emergency response, event management, human rights, disability access, and security— my books are filled with true stories (bridezillas), worst-case scenarios (malfunctioning zippers), and my favorite tropes (one-bed).

I'm a strong proponent of #OwnVoices, and specialize in fiercely inclusive happily ever afters.

ALSO BY EVIE MITCHELL

All Access Series

Knot My Type

Love Flushed

Darn Knit All

Larsson Siblings

Thunder Thighs

Clean Sweep

The X-List

Reality Check

The A-List

Capricorn Cove

The Shake-up

Double the D

Muffin Top

The Mrs. Clause

New Year, Knew You

Double Breasted

As You Wish

You Sleigh Me

Meat Load

Resolution Revolution

Dogg Pack

Puppy Love

Bad English

The Frock Up

Pier Pressure

Trick or Trent

New Year's Faye

Reigning Hearts

The Marriage Claim

Silent Knight

Men of Trinity Bay

Kink in the Road

Nameless Souls MC

Runner

Wrath

Ghost

Shield

Elliot Security

Rough Edge

Bleeding Edge

www.ingramcontent.com/pod-product-compliance
Lightning Source LLC
Chambersburg PA
CBHW010021200726
48283CB00015B/3252